CW01522257

Joseph Smith Fletcher

THE GREAT BRIGHTON

MYSTERY

Elibron Classics
www.elibron.com

Elibron Classics series.

© 2006 Adamant Media Corporation.

ISBN 0-543-90292-7 (paperback)
ISBN 0-543-90291-9 (hardcover)

Elibron and Elibron Classics are trademarks of
Adamant Media Corporation. All rights reserved.

This book is an accurate reproduction of the original. Any marks, names, colophons, imprints, logos or other symbols or identifiers that appear on or in this book, except for those of Adamant Media Corporation and BookSurge, LLC, are used only for historical reference and accuracy and are not meant to designate origin or imply any sponsorship by or license from any third party.

Chapter I
The Dead Man at Black Rock

On the eastern confines of Brighton, near the rapidly-changing point of headland called Black Rock, there are still left on the crumbling cliffs a certain diminishing number of old-world dwellings which were there, probably, in the days when George the Third was king and Dr. Johnson and Fanny Burney knew the now populous and fashionable seaside resort as a little fishing village called Brighthelmstone. These dwellings are affairs of substantial stone, thick walled and heavily roofed; they have weathered storms against which the high chalk cliffs on which they are perched have not been able to hold out. The erosion of wind and wave have been at work on these cliffs for centuries, and now some of the ancient cottages and farmsteads are on the edge of the headland from which they were once well separated; here and there, close by, you may trace the remains of other dwellings which were gradually undermined by erosion and finally fell to the beach beneath. Eventually all the old houses that are left will go, too; still, there are folk in them who think that their time will not be just yet, and who sleep o' nights undisturbed by the fear of the tides that beat warningly below: one of these folk, a few years ago, was an elderly man named Hopperson.

Hopperson had spent most of his life at sea; he was known to his neighbours as an ex-petty officer of the Royal Navy; a smart, bright-eyed, cheery little man, retired on a pension, and inclined to make the most of the days remaining to him. His naval training and career had made Hopperson a man of rule and method, and given him a distinct hatred of idleness; accordingly his time was carefully mapped out; person of leisure though he was, he always had something to do, not merely for himself but for his neighbours. He was a great hand at mending and improving, and could transform himself from a plumber to an upholsterer, from a carpenter to a paperhanger as readily as he could shift a tool from his left to his right hand. If he was not found to be at one of these jobs in his own house, you would be sure to find him busy at another in somebody else's. Apart from these tricks of making himself useful to his own and the surrounding families, Hopperson had some habits, out of which nothing could shake him. One was to go out of his door, as soon as he was dressed in the morning, armed with an old telescope, with which, from a point on the cliff just beneath his cottage, he carefully swept land, sea and sky in every direction — just, he said, to see how the world was looking. He usually spent half an hour in this pursuit; at the end of it, he would close his telescope with a snap and go indoors to eat his breakfast.

As a rule Hopperson saw nothing more remarkable in these morning inspections than ships going up and down Channel, steamers crossing to and from France, and the opaline mists circling along the coast and on the crest of the downs behind him. But one autumn morning, when there was more than a touch of frost in the air, and the atmosphere was unusually clear, Hopperson suddenly saw something which stiffened the arms holding the telescope and made him stare hard and keen through the polished glasses. He had been following the line of the beach at the foot of the cliffs that run eastward towards Rottingdean; it was an object lying in that line which arrested his attention, and the object appeared, at first, to be a big, black bundle, showing distinct and bold against the chalk. A bundle, as it were, of old clothes... but within another minute Hopperson knew it was not that. The black thing was the crumpled-up, motionless body of a man.

Close by where Hopperson stood there was a steep pathway leading down to the beach, and he closed his telescope hastily and made equal haste to descend. Once on the beach he hurried towards the motionless heap; before he reached it he knew that it was lifeless; its very stillness was eloquent of that. Presently he stood by it — the body of a man of something a little over middle age; a tall, rather heavily built man; from his dress and general appearance, a gentleman. He lay in an attitude which convinced Hopperson that he had never moved from where he had fallen, and Hopperson had no doubt as to the cause of his death. He had fallen from the edge of the high chalk cliff above — a fall of some fifty or sixty feet — and he had broken his neck and died instantly. When Hopperson had laid his hand on the man's cheek, he knew that death had taken place many hours before; probably in the darkness of the previous evening.

From his intimate knowledge of the district, Hopperson easily deduced a conclusion as to how this accident had happened. All along the edge of the cliffs at that point was a narrow footpath. Once upon a time that footpath had been many yards away from the actual edge; now, because of the gradual wearing down of the cliffs by erosion, there were places where it was close to the edge, only a few inches from the edge... and there were other places, in the line of the footpath, where it did not exist at all — gaps. Anyone following that path at night and coming to one of those gaps — wholly unprotected — would inevitably crash down to the pebbly beach beneath and to sure death. Folk who lived about there never used that path, of course, and strangers were not likely to know of its existence.. Hopperson, realising this, made another hasty deduction — this man, presumably a visitor to Brighton, had known that path years ago, when it was still safe, and believing it to be in its previous condition, had turned into it at a point farther along the headlands — with the result that he now lay at Hopperson's feet, dead.

Hopperson was remembering that the previous evening and early night had been unusually dark, even for that time of year, when he heard approaching footsteps, and looking round saw one of his neighbours, a fisherman, coming along the shingle. The man had evidently caught sight of him and of the motionless heap before him, and was hurrying. Hopperson accelerated his movements with a beckoning hand.

"Here's a sad affair, Elsworth!" he said in hushed tones. "Gentleman fallen from the top there — last night, I should say. Dead? — oh, yes, he's dead enough, poor fellow! — been dead a good while, too. Haven't I said many a time and oft that that headland ought to be fenced in? — aye, I knew there'd be an accident some day. Well! — there's nothing to do but to get the police. Run round to the nearest telephone, Elsworth, and let them know at the Town Hall — tell them to send an ambulance up. And if you see our policeman about, tell him. I'll stay here."

Elsworth, after a glance at the dead man and a muttered comment on the dangerous path, ran off towards the nearest house, and Hopperson, left alone with the silent and motionless figure, looked more closely at it. After his first laying of a hand on the dead man's face he made no offer to touch man or clothing; he had a notion, common to the people, that if you find a dead body, you must not handle it. But he noted that from his appearance and attire this man was probably a very well-to-do man: one of those rich men who haunt palatial hotels in the season. Everything about him betokened wealth: his smart overcoat had been forced open by his fall, and Hopperson caught a glimpse of an equally smart tweed suit beneath, and of a heavy gold watch-chain across the waistcoat. Trained to observe little things, he also noted the dead man's glossy linen, the diamond pin in his cravat, the expensive shoes and gaiters on his feet — a bit of a dandy this had been, he thought. And close by lay, on one hand, a gold-mounted umbrella, and on the other, a Homburg hat: Hopperson picked up the hat and glanced at the name of its maker, a fashionable hatter in the West End of London. He looked more closely into the lining; some men, he knew, make a practice of having their names or initials stamped or written inside their hats. But here there was nothing of that sort: all that Hopperson gathered was that the hat was a new one.

Hopperson knew that some little time must elapse before the police came: the nearest telephone to which Elsworth could go was at a grocer's shop, half a mile away. He began to move about — the morning was cold; an east wind came cuttingly along the foot of the cliffs. As he moved, he kept his eyes open for signs or traces of anything relating to the accident. He fancied that he saw a breakage in the face of the slightly shelving headland, as if the dead man had clutched at it in his fall; that, of course, and the surface of the cliff immediately above, would in due course be investigated by the police. But around the body there was nothing unusual: Hopperson came to the conclusion that the man had plunged head foremost from above and had never stirred from where he fell. The actual bit of shore on which he had fallen was of hard rock and banked-up shingle, well removed from high-water mark; nobody, reflected Hopperson, could have crashed down on that and lived, especially anyone of this man's heavy build.

Walking round and round, beating his arms across his chest to keep himself warm, Hopperson suddenly caught sight of an object which, with the sailor's instinct of picking up and keeping anything that may come in useful, he lifted from the pebbles and slipped into the deep inner pocket of his pea-jacket. This was a steel spanner, of some size for such things, twelve or fifteen inches in length; the sort of tool used for screwing on big nuts. It was worn and rusted; Hopperson's notion of it was that it was no more than a bit of the sort of jetsam that one finds thrown up on every coast: he would throw it in his tool-box when he went home and perhaps clean it up some day. He never thought of it in connection with the accident, and when the police came half an hour later he never as much as mentioned it. Hopperson, indeed, had completed his theory about the strange gentleman's death before the police drew near. When they came — half a dozen of them, including a man in plain clothes, who turned out to be a detective — he told them his theory, that this gentleman had probably known that cliff footpath years ago, had followed it on the previous evening, believing it to be safe, and had fallen at the break in the headland above them.

Credding, the detective, asked Hopperson to show him the nearest way to the top of the cliff; Hopperson conducted him there by the path near the point from which he had caught sight of the dead man. Arrived at the gap into which the stranger had fallen, Credding nodded his head — acknowledging the truth of the suggestions Hopperson had made as they went up.

"Just as you say," he remarked. "The path comes to a sharp end on both sides this gap. What astonishes me is that any man should have been so foolish as to walk so near the extreme edge of this cliff! Unbelievable!"

"When I first came to live here," said Hopperson, "this path was at least fifteen yards from the edge of the cliff. And that's not so many years ago! The coast's wearing away faster than anybody knows' about here."

"But you'd think anybody could see!" answered Credding. "Surely, if you were walking along here of a night, you'd see the line of the headland —"

"Last night was unusually dark," said Hopperson. "I noticed it. I was out, near my cottage, about eight, and again about ten-thirty. It was a very dark night. And —" He paused, checked by a movement on the part of his companion. Credding, after going as near the extreme edge of the cliff as he dared, was now retreating inland, bending closely to the close-textured turf. Suddenly he looked up, pointing to a continuous line or scratch in the grass which Hopperson saw plainly.

"Looks to me," he said, "as if something sharp has been dragged over that. It's a distinct mark, anyway — and newly made."

Hopperson offered no comment. He knew nothing of the detective's idea, and when he presently followed him down to the beach he was still confident that the dead man had come. to his end by an accidental fall. But Credding, rejoining the others, went straight to the body, and lifted, first the left, then the right foot. His glance, when he looked up, was directed, to Hopperson.

"Look at this!" he said, "in relation to that mark on the grass up there. Do you see — this man's evidently been inclined to walk a bit heavier on the right foot than on the left, and his bootmaker's remedied that by putting a bit of steel plate underneath the right heel — here it is. And, see — it's loose, and projects! That accounts very likely for that line on the grass. I think this man was struck down up there, stunned, probably, and then thrown over the cliff."

"That would be — murder!" exclaimed Hopperson, aghast.

"What else?" said Credding. "And look at that," he went on, pointing to an ugly contusion on the dead man's left temple. "That doesn't look as if it had been caused by falling on these pebbles — it looks more like a blow. However, we'd better get him down to the mortuary, and let the doctors see him. You'd just as well come along with us," he concluded, turning to Hopperson. "They'll want all the information they can get, down there."

Hopperson followed to the town: he was present while the doctors examined the dead man and the police searched his clothing. The doctors said little, except that the man had been dead at least twelve hours: about the contusion on the temple they would say nothing at all; it seemed to Hopperson that they were gravely reticent. He turned his attention to the things which a policeman turned out of the dead man's pockets — money in considerable quantity, a fine gold watch and chain, an equally valuable cigar-case and match-box; it was evident, muttered an official standing by, that if there had been foul play it was not for purposes of robbery. But there were no letters or papers, and the man's identity remained a mystery until the searching fingers drew from a waistcoat pocket a bit of printed card.

"Hotel ticket," announced the searcher. "Room No. 81, Grand International Hotel." He turned to another man. "Ring up the Grand International, Jim," he said. "Ask 'em to send their reception clerk along."

Hopperson waited another quarter of an hour. Nobody took any notice of him as he sat in a corner of the room. The two doctors were whispering in another corner; in the centre the police were discussing matters amongst themselves. At last a young man came hurrying in — to be led up to the dead man. He gave the body one glance and nodded confidently.

"Oh, yes," he said. "I know him! Mr. Martin Severfield. Registered at our hotel yesterday afternoon — three o'clock. Yes! That's Mr. Severfield — right enough!"

Chapter II
The Dead Man's Solicitor

Credding, whom Hopperson had already set down as a person of importance and who appeared to have assumed the direction of inquiries about this affair, began to question the reception clerk. But the reception clerk knew nothing, or next to nothing. He could give no information as to Mr. Severfield's movements subsequent to his arrival at the Grand International Hotel; he didn't know if he had dined there the previous evening, nor if he had occupied the room which he had booked; all he knew was that he had booked a room, and that he had entered his address in the register as "Savoy Hotel, London." Nor could he say if Mr. Severfield had ever been at the Grand International before — he, at any rate, had no recollection of him.

"I don't think he's an Englishman," he added, glancing at the dead man. "Didn't give me the impression that he was, anyway; I took him for an American, or a Colonial, or something of that sort. I think he only meant staying a night — he'd no luggage but a small suit-case."

"I'll go back with you to the hotel," said Credding. "You say he gave the Savoy as his London address? — all right, we'll communicate with the management there at once. Just get on the 'phone with the Savoy, in London," he went on, turning to another official. "Give them the facts, and ask what they know of Mr. Martin Severfield, and if he's any relatives there. You'll have heard by the time I'm back — I'll go round and see what's to be picked up the Grand International."

As he left the room Credding caught sight of Hopperson, and paused.

"Oh — yes," he said. "I don't think you need wait any longer, Mr. Hopperson. Of course, you're aware that there'll have to be an inquest, and that you'll be wanted at it? — we'll let you know about that. There's nothing more you can tell me just now, I suppose?"

"No — I think you know all that I know," answered Hopperson. He lingered uneasily, glancing at the doctors, still talking together. "Do — do you think it's been murder, then, Mr. Credding?" he asked. "Not — accidental?"

"We shall know more as to that in good time," replied Credding. "If you hear anything up your way — such as that this gentleman was seen about that quarter last night, or anything of that sort — let us know at once. Keep your ears open — a stray word or two's useful, you know."

He nodded and made off with the reception clerk, and Hopperson went home, full of news for his wife and hungry for his breakfast. But before he sat down he went into his little workshop and, taking the spanner from his side-pocket, threw it into a box in which lay a collection of similar things, picked up here and there; to that spanner Hopperson attached no importance — it was just a bit of rusted steel, a come-by-chance; he had never even thought of it when Credding asked if there was anything more he could tell.

While Hopperson was pouring out his budget of news to his astonished spouse, Credding was busy making inquiries at the Grand International Hotel. Of one fact he quickly became assured — the late Mr. Martin Severfield was a stranger, not merely to the hotel, but to Brighton. His movements, after his arrival at the Grand International about three o'clock the previous afternoon, were easy to trace — up to a certain point. After being shown up to his room, he had come down again, and at the entrance had asked the hall-porter certain questions about the town which proved that he had never been in it before. He had then gone out, and had been seen to return about six o'clock. From that time until seven, Mr. Severfield had been in one of the smoking-rooms, where a waiter had served him with a glass or two of dry sherry. Shortly after seven he had entered the dining-room; the waiter who had attended to him there remembered him quite well, and said that he sat some time over his solitary dinner; it had been past eight o'clock when he left his table. The next information about him came from the hall-porter; Mr. Severfield, he said, had passed him at the door at about ten minutes after eight; he was wearing an overcoat and carrying an umbrella, and he turned along the front towards the east. He was alone; he seemed always to have been alone; no one in the hotel had seen him in conversation with any other guest. And after he had walked away from the hotel, nobody had seen him again until the reception clerk saw him lying dead at the mortuary.

Credding went up to the dead man's room. It was still early in the morning, and the chambermaids were flitting about the corridors; the manager, accompanying the detective, quickly summoned the one in charge of Number 81. She opened Number 81 with her key; everything was in order there — but there were no signs of occupancy during the preceding night; the bed had not been slept in. And all that the chambermaid knew was that at seven o'clock the previous evening the gentleman of Number 81 had come up there for a few minutes — she had seen him washing his hands and brushing his hair, for he had left the door half open while he was in the room, and she had passed and re-passed — and had then gone down again; since then she had never seen him.

"Seems pretty evident," said Credding to the manager, "that he never returned to the hotel after your hall-porter saw him go out at eight-ten. Well, this, I suppose, is his suit-case, and I'll just examine it. Not that I expect to find anything of any note."

The manager stood by while Credding opened the case, which was unlocked. There was nothing in it that afforded any clue as to the cause of the death of its owner. A brand new suit of tweed — made by a fashionable West End tailoring firm. Linen. Handkerchiefs. Socks. A couple of magazines. A book. A soft travelling cap. Innocent things, all — equally innocent were the other things arranged about the room — a suit of gaily-coloured pyjamas on the bed; a pair of shoes and a pair of slippers on the hearthrug; toilet necessaries on the dressing-table; more on the washstand. And on the chest of drawers a folded copy of yesterday's *Times* and a box of cigars. The manager saw nothing but the obvious in these things, and he glanced inquisitively at Credding when the detective took up *The Times* and, unfolding it, began to study certain advertisement columns.

"Just so," said Credding, answering the look of inquiry. "I was wondering if there was anything here that had brought this Mr. Severfield to Brighton — an advertisement of, say, property to sell, a house to let, anything of that sort. Because, as a rule, a man who's been reading *The Times* on a journey, leaves it behind him in his railway carriage; he doesn't fold it neatly and bring it to his hotel bedroom. However — I see nothing there."

He presently went away from the Grand International and slowly back towards police head-quarters. And on the way he met one of the doctors whom he had left still bending over the dead man. The two men paused at sight of each other, and drew aside on the pavement.

"Come to any conclusion?" asked Credding abruptly.

The doctor hesitated.

"We're not sure about that mark on the man's forehead," he answered at last. "We're not satisfied that it was caused by the fall. It looks more like the sort of contusion you'd get from a heavy blow with some blunt weapon."

"Would it cause death — that blow?" asked Credding.

"I don't think so," replied the doctor. "Unconsciousness, certainly. There are other, more serious injuries, of course. The man's neck was broken."

"Real cause of death, that, I suppose?" suggested the detective. "Still, I wish you could decide definitely about that contusion, doctor. If the man fell down the cliffs, his death's due to accident; if somebody first struck him and then threw the body over, it's murder!"

"I'll let you know later," said the doctor. "Find anything out at the hotel?"

"Next to nothing," replied Credding. "He went out of that just after dinner last night and never returned. A stranger there. However, we shall hear something —"

He went on to head-quarters and sought the man whom he had instructed to telephone to London; at sight of him the man produced two memoranda.

"Heard from the Savoy people," he said. "I jotted it down. They reply that Mr. Martin Severfield's an Australian gentleman, who's had a suite of rooms at their hotel for some months past — very wealthy man. Left there yesterday morning, saying he was going to Brighton for the night, and should be back next day, or possibly day after. No idea why he visited Brighton. They've communicated our news to Mr. Severfield's solicitor, and to his bankers. And there's a message here from the solicitor — Mr. Leicester Colinrake, of Southampton Street, Strand. Nothing but that he's just heard news from the Savoy people, and he's leaving for Brighton immediately."

"If he comes while I'm out," said Credding, "tell him I shan't be long, and keep him here till I get back. I'm just going up to Black Rock for ten minutes."

But before Credding left head-quarters, there was a thing to be done, on the doing of which he had been meditating ever since meeting the doctor with whom he had had his conversation about the contusion of Severfield's temple. By this time, Severfield's body had been laid out and his clothing folded and put away in safety. Credding went and got the shoes and, putting them in a handbag, chartered a taxicab and rode along to Black Rock; already he was convinced that the footprint question might possibly be a big one in this case.

The news of the tragedy — murder or accident — had spread fast all round that neighbourhood, and when Credding reached the cliff there were scores of people on it, and scores more on the beach below. But he had foreseen this, and before leaving the place earlier in the morning had stationed policemen there with instructions to keep curious sightseers away from two particular areas — one, the land immediately surrounding the gap through which Severfield had either fallen or been thrown; the other, the strip of rocky and shingly beach on which he had crashed. It was to the upper area that he first gave his attention. The actual gap was a V-shaped break in the line of the cliffs; the path came to the outer lines of this V on either side, and on each, of course, terminated abruptly. Anyone walking along that path in the darkness, and coming to the gap, would go headlong to the beach beneath — that was a dead-sure thing, muttered Credding to himself. And, as he had remarked to Hopperson, on first seeing the place, he could not understand how any man could be so foolish as to follow that path. What he now wanted to know was — had anyone followed it? For on that point Credding already had strong doubts.

The path itself was a narrow, grassless affair of trodden earth, with a surface of plastic mud, so soft that the least pressure made a clear impression in it. Walking alongside it, on the short, wiry grass that bounded it, Credding followed it for some distance on either side the gap. And he saw at once what some intuition had led him to believe he would see. There was no doubt whatever about it — *nowhere along that path, on left or right of the gap, was there the single mark of a recent footstep.* However

Severfield had come to the gap, it had not been by walking to it along the disused path. That was certain.

There was an old man standing near, who watched the detective's doings with silent and respectful attention. Credding turned to him.

"Live hereabouts?" he asked.

The old man pointed his stick to the nearest cottages.

"Lived in one o' those a matter of seventy year, master," he answered.

"Then you know these parts," said Credding. "Nobody ever uses this path nowadays, eh?"

"Not us about here, master!" replied the old man. "Us knows the danger on it too well, us do! Time was when there was a good twenty yards 'twixt that there path and the edge o' the cliff, but for a long time 't has been as you do see it — a man-trap, I calls it. For them as don't know, that is. No — I ain't seen nobody a-follerin' o' that path this many a year."

Credding looked round. Landward, a narrow, sloping field of grass lay between the points at which he was standing, close by the gap, and the high road which leads from Brighton to Rottingdean. Beyond the high road was more sloping ground, whereon were certain buildings, private houses, cottages, an old farmstead or two. He began to formulate theories, glancing at the mark in the turf which he had pointed out to Hopperson. Supposing Severfield, for some reason or other at which he, Credding, could not even guess, had been struck down in one of those houses across there, and that his body had then been dragged across the sloping field down to this gap, to be there flung over to the beach? Possible... anyway, he was certain of one fact — Severfield had not approached that gap by the path, in either direction. And having settled that point to his own complete satisfaction, Credding, without opening the bag in which he had carried the dead man's shoes, went back to head-quarters.

He found Mr. Leicester Colinrake talking with an inspector; Mr. Colinrake had arrived from London ten minutes previously: a man of about thirty-five years of age, whose appearance was that of a smart military man rather than of a man of law. He had just identified Severfield, and seemed to be greatly concerned by the suddenness of his death.

"Mr. Severfield was at my office at noon yesterday," he said. "In fact, we had an early lunch together, before he left for Brighton. I couldn't credit the news they sent me on from the Savoy — in fact, I don't think I really did believe it until — well, until just now. Now, of course —"

He ended with an expressive gesture, and as neither Credding nor the inspector made any remark, he went on.

"This is a most lamentable affair!" he said, shaking his head. "You will want, of course, to know all I can tell you about Mr. Severfield. He'd been a client of mine for several months. He was a man of considerable wealth — great wealth, which he'd acquired in various parts of the world. Now it was his intention to settle down in England. And — the saddest feature of this! — he was just about to be married!"

Chapter III
Who was the Lady?

Up to then Credding had made no offer to join in the conversation that had been going on when he entered the room: he had remained standing near the mantelpiece, taking stock of Colinrake. But now he sat down, as if to listen at his leisure.

"I should like to hear all you can tell about this Mr. Severfield," he said. "Of course, being his solicitor, you're in a position to know."

"A good deal, certainly," replied Colinrake. "I can tell all I know of him since he came to me some months — eight or nine months — ago. He called on me about a conveyancing matter — some property he'd bought — and from that time I began to see him regularly — in fact, he gave me all his legal business — not much of it, but what he had. We became very friendly; he didn't know many people here and I think he was glad of my society. As I believe you're already aware, he'd a suite of rooms at the Savoy Hotel — an expensive suite."

"Rich man, eh?" suggested Credding.

"A very wealthy man — very!" assented Colinrake. "He told me bits about himself. I fancy — he was never very explicit about his earlier career — that he went out to Australia in his young days, and made money there. But he'd had business dealings in various countries — China, India, South Africa, the Argentine, and he'd certainly lived some little time in New Orleans. He'd more interests than one — I don't think he'd any particular line of business; as far as I could make out he had capital invested in all sorts of ventures. And anyway, he'd come to England to settle down. He was going to buy a country house — he and I had been on the look-out for the right sort of property for some little time. He was the sort of man who likes country life — shooting, fishing, hunting: that sort of thing. We had one or two likely places in view, in the Midlands. A country gentleman's life, you know — that was what he wanted. He was, I believe, gradually retiring all his capital from his various holdings in the countries I've mentioned, and was re-investing it here; I fancy he'd large amounts lying at his bankers, in the City. That he was looking forward to a definitely settled life here, I know. And that is — well, that's really about all I can tell!"

"Good general account, Mr. Colinrake," said Credding. "But — there are little details that may be important. To start with — do you know if Mr. Severfield had any relations?"

"He hadn't," replied Colinrake promptly. "He told me, soon after we first met, that he hadn't a near relation in the world, and that if he'd any distant ones, he didn't even know their names! He was a lonely man. What's more, he'd got used to loneliness. I wanted him to join one or two clubs in town, but he'd no taste that way. He had hobbies — he was a bit of a picture collector, and he'd a liking for old books and old china. But — he wasn't a social sort."

"You say you saw him yesterday morning," continued Credding. "Do you know why he came to Brighton?"

"No, I don't. He told me he was going to run down here, for a day, or possibly a day or two, but he didn't tell me why, and I didn't ask him," replied Colinrake. "There was nothing unusual in his coming here — he was given to going off for a day or so to places — just to have a look at them. He knew next to nothing of England — I think he'd left it as a mere boy."

For the last few minutes, Credding, while listening attentively to all that the solicitor was saying, had been making shorthand notes in a small pocket-book. But on the head of the page on which he had begun making them he had written a date in longhand: *Tuesday, October 17th,* 1922, and had drawn a line under it. That date represented to Credding the start-out of this affair — as far as he was concerned.

He looked up from his book, suddenly, and put a question to Colinrake which made the solicitor start.

"You don't know of any reason to cause Severfield to commit suicide?" he asked.

Colinrake shook his head with vehement assertion.

"Suicide? Severfield?" he exclaimed. "Good heavens, no! Last man in the world! Why should he commit suicide? Only just middle-aged and looking and feeling younger than his years — rich — in good health — the best of health — and just about to be married! — Good Lord, why, he'd everything to live for! And in his way — a quiet way — he was fond of life!"

"Just so!" said Credding imperturbably. "Not likely to commit suicide, eh? Very well — and now about this contemplated marriage. Who —"

Before he could complete his question the door opened, and a constable came in with a card which he handed to the inspector. He, glancing at the name, read it aloud.

" 'Mr. Robert Bridgwater, 91, Cadogan Gardens'?" he said. "Who's he?"

"Severfield's banker," answered Colinrake promptly. "Bridgwater, Massiter, and Bridgwater, Lombard Street. Big private bankers, with a lot of foreign business. You'd better see him."

"Oh, of course!" responded the inspector. "Show Mr. Bridgwater in," he added, turning to the constable. "I suppose you know him, Mr. Colinrake?"

"No — not personally," replied Colinrake. "Only by sight. I heard from the Savoy people that they'd telephoned the news to Bridgwater, though. They're evidently deeply concerned about it, or Mr. Bridgwater wouldn't have come down here."

Mr. Bridgwater came hurrying in — a big, elderly man with a keen, business-like face and manner; his sharp, observant eyes looked swiftly from one to the other of the three men who had risen to meet him, until they fastened on the uniformed inspector.

"I came here as soon as I got the news of Mr. Severfield's death," he said hastily, "and without waiting for any further particulars. Is it true that he is dead? And that there's no mistake about his identity?"

"Quite true, sir," answered the inspector. "And he's been identified by this gentleman — Mr. Colinrake, his solicitor."

The banker gave Colinrake one of his sharp looks and a nod.

"I've heard of you, Mr. Colinrake — from him, of course," he said. "Dear, dear! — this is a most distressing affair. An accident, eh? Fell over the cliffs, I understand?"

The inspector pointed to Credding.

"This is Detective-Sergeant Credding, Mr. Bridgwater," he said. "He's in charge of the investigations — as far as they've gone. And perhaps you'd like to see the body —"

Credding motioned Bridgwater to follow him, and led him to the mortuary. There, after a pause, he pointed out to the banker the contusion on the dead man's forehead.

"That's the doubtful thing, sir," he whispered. "The medical men — our police-surgeon and another doctor — are not satisfied about it. They're inclined to think that that blow was inflicted by some heavy, blunt instrument, before death. In that case — it looks like murder."

The banker drew in his breath sharply. He turned away to the door, and he and Credding went outside.

"I spotted that mark on his temple as soon as I saw him," remarked Credding. "It made me suspicious, at once."

"But — but he did fall over the cliffs, didn't he?" asked Bridgwater.

"He fell over the cliffs, certainly — a bad fall," assented Credding. "And his neck was broken. But — he may have been thrown over. Personally, I'm inclined to think he was thrown over. I'll tell you why, sir," — he proceeded to give the banker a circumstantial account of his investigations so far — "I think, you see," he concluded, "that he may have been struck and stunned somewhere near that point, possibly in some house, then dragged to the gap I've told you of, and flung down to the beach, the murderers — for I don't think one man could have dragged him — believing that it would be thought that he had fallen over by accident. Of course, that's supposition on my part. But — I have certain grounds for it, as I've explained. When you came in just now, Mr. Bridgwater, Mr. Colinrake was telling us all he knew about Mr. Severfield. Perhaps you know more? Do you know if he had enemies, for instance?"

"No!" replied Bridgwater promptly. "I don't! But I know little of his private affairs."

"He was a man who'd had big business interests, I understand?" asked Credding.

"A very wealthy man?"

The banker shook his head as if to emphasise the gravity of his words.

"He was a very wealthy man indeed!" he answered with evident meaning. "I — the fact is, we have an enormous sum of money lying to his credit — and I haven't the faintest notion who his relations are!"

"Mr. Colinrake says he told him that he had none — no near ones, at any rate," remarked Credding, "and that if he had any distant ones, he didn't know anything about them. So —"

The constable who had ushered Bridgwater into the inspector's room came along a corridor and caught sight of the detective and the banker in conversation. He beckoned to Credding. "There's a man just come in — Simpson, a taxicab driver — who wants to tell something about this Black Rock affair," he said. "I've taken him to the room where you were talking — they want you there."

Credding hurried his companion back to the room they had recently quitted. There, seated on a chair between the inspector and Colinrake, was a young man whom Credding recognised as a cabman often seen along the front near the principal hotels. He was in his driver's dress, and held his peaked cap in one hand — waiting. And in the other hand he held what Credding saw to be a special edition of the local paper.

"This man's got some information to give, Credding," said the inspector, as he handed Bridgwater a chair. "I told him to wait till you came back."

"What is it, Simpson?" inquired Credding. "I know you — you're one of Watley's men, aren't you?"

"That's so, sir," replied Simpson. He held up the paper. "This here, Mr. Credding," he went on. "It's got a piece in about this affair discovered at Black Rock this morning — the gentleman as fell over the cliffs and killed himself. Well, sir, I'm pretty positive I drove that gentleman last night!"

"Is there any description of him then in the paper?" asked Credding.

"Yes, sir," answered Simpson. "A good description. It was that —"

"We gave a full description to the press first thing," interrupted the inspector. "It'll be that, of course."

"Well?" said Credding. "Go on, Simpson. Tell what you know."

"This here, sir. I'm as certain as I can be that I drove this here gentleman — as described in the paper — last night. He's put down here in the paper — looks and clothes — just as I remember him. I drove him to the end of Ovingdean Lane."

"Alone?" asked Credding.

"No, sir. He'd a lady with him!"

The men listening glanced at each other. Here was a new element introduced into the story. And Credding, who had been standing, dropped into a chair and produced his little notebook.

"Tell the whole thing in your own way, Simpson — from the start," he said. "Go ahead!"

"Well, sir, like this — I was with my cab at the corner of East Street at about twenty past eight last night. This here gentleman comes up with a lady — they'd come walking along the front, past the Queen's Hotel, sir. They stopped when they got to me, and said something to each other. Then he beckoned me, and they got into my cab — she got in first, of course. He told me to drive 'em to the end of Ovingdean Lane, and to stop there. I did. They got out, and he paid me. Didn't ask how much it was, neither. He give me three half-dollars, as a matter o' fact. And he said I needn't wait. I left 'em there — they was at the side of the road, where the lane turns up to Ovingdean, talking. And — that's all, Mr. Credding."

"Scarcely!" said the detective. "There's a lot more than that, my lad! First, did you get a good view of the gentleman's face?"

"Yes, sir — full view of him in the lamplight, corner of East Street."

"You shall have a look at him again, presently. Well — did you get a good look at the lady?"

"No, sir — no, Mr. Credding! Never see her face at all!"

"Why not?"

" 'Cause she'd one o' these here veils on, sir, what you can't see through! And muffled up all about her neck and chin, too — couldn't see nothing!"

"Well, what sort of woman was she, otherwise, as far as you could see?"

"Talish lady — well made — active in her movements — got into the cab spry enough, anyhow, sir."

"How was she dressed, Simpson?"

"Up to the mark, sir! Furs — that sort o' thing. Quite the fashionable lady, Mr. Credding! — I knows 'em when I see 'em. Patent shiny leather shoes. Swell!"

"You see a lot of fashionable ladies, Simpson — naturally. Drive 'em about, don't you? Do you remember seeing this lady — as far as you could recognise her by her swell clothes — before?"

"No, sir — no, I'm sure I never had. I'm a good head at that sort o' thing, too, Mr. Credding — I take stock o' ladies' fine clothes. No — she was an utter stranger to me."

Credding rose, and beckoning the taxicab driver to follow him, led him to the mortuary, and drew aside the sheet from the, dead man's face.

"Now, Simpson," he whispered. "Take a good look! And — don't make any mistake!"

"That's him, Mr. Credding!" said Simpson, in a hushed voice. "Oh, yes, sir!"

"You're certain?"

"Take my 'davy on it!" answered Simpson stoutly. "Oh, yes, Mr. Credding, dead sure! That's the gentleman I've been talking about — his very self!"

Credding replaced the sheet. This was the man, then. But — who and where was the woman?

Chapter IV
Find Out!

The detective sent Simpson away, with an admonition to keep his tongue quiet till he was told to speak, and went back to the room where he had left the other men. He dropped into a chair and glanced meaningly at the inspector.

"That's all right," he said quietly. "He recognised him!"

"Certain about it?" asked the inspector.

"Dead certain!" affirmed Credding. He turned to Colinrake. "You told us, just before Mr. Bridgwater came in, that Severfield was about to be married. Do you think this lady who was with him last night could be the one he was to be married to?"

"No!" exclaimed Colinrake sharply. "I'm sure she wasn't!"

"Why?" asked Credding.

"Because," replied Colinrake, "I saw that lady last night, myself, in London, about eight o'clock."

"That's conclusive, of course," remarked Credding. "Well, we shall have to get busy about Severfield's movements in Brighton. He was out of his hotel for two or three hours in the afternoon — we must find out where he went, what he did, if anybody had any dealings with him, and so on. But meanwhile, as we want to know all we can about him, and as you're here, and as Mr. Bridgwater's here, perhaps you'll give us what help you can. This proposed marriage, now —"

"I was not aware that Mr. Severfield was about to be married," said the banker. "In fact, I'm surprised to hear it! To be sure, I haven't seen him very lately, but I did see him about — say three weeks ago, and he didn't mention his marriage to me. And we have been on pretty friendly and intimate terms!"

"It was not definitely arranged three weeks ago," said Colinrake. "He became engaged about a fortnight since, and the marriage was to take place very soon. Mr. Severfield," he added, after a moment's pause, "was the sort of man who didn't care for delay — once an arrangement had been made."

Bridgwater made no remark: it seemed to Credding that he was considerably taken aback by the announcement of the forthcoming marriage. And Credding quietly produced his little note-book again.

"Well, Mr. Colinrake can give us all the details," he re-marked. "Who is the lady, Mr. Colinrake?"

"This will be very painful news for her," said Colinrake. "I shall have to get back to town and break the news. The lady is a Miss Greville, Miss Beatrix Greville. Severfield was very much in love with her. A — a quite romantic affair!"

"I gather from what you say that Miss Greville is a youthful lady," remarked Credding, with a certain half-ironical note which was not lost on the banker. "Not a lady of Mr. Severfield's own age, eh?"

Miss Greville is a young lady of, I fancy, about twenty-two or three," answered Colinrake. "And one of remarkable charm and ability, and I may say, character. Her father was a client of mine; dead, now." He rose, looking at his watch. "I must go," he continued. "I've only just time to get my train back to town. Of course, I shall be back here for the inquest. In the meantime, if there's anything you want me for, and if you've anything to tell me, ring me up on the phone."

He murmured his adieux, and was hastening to the door when the banker stopped him.

"A moment, Mr. Colinrake — and a question," he said. "Do you know if Mr. Severfield has left a will?"

"Yes!" answered Colinrake promptly. "He has! I have it."

"Do you know its provisions?"

"I do. Mr. Severfield has left practically everything he pos-sessed to the lady I have just spoken of — Miss Greville."

"Everything?"

"He had no relations, Mr. Bridgwater! Yes — everything! All is in order — I shall produce the will at the proper time."

"And — trustees or executors?" asked the banker. "What about that?"

"Miss Greville is named as sole executor," answered Colin-rake hurriedly. "Excuse me — I must go. I want to get to town before Miss Greville and her aunt, with whom she lives, hear of this through the London evening papers."

He went off without further ceremony, and Credding closed his book and slipped it quietly into his pocket.

"Um!" he said. "Well — that's something!"

Bridgwater looked more closely at the detective: up to that point he had not given much attention to him. Credding was a very ordinary looking little man, approaching middle-age; rosy-cheeked, plump-figured; he cultivated old-fashioned mutton-chop whiskers and wore clothes of a sporting sort; if he had not known that he was a detective, the banker would have set him down as a butcher with a taste for horse-racing. But now that he looked at him more closely he saw a remarkable shrewdness in Credding's eyes, and a certain determination about his clean-shaven lips and chin — this was a man, he said to himself, who, if he took a job in hand, would go through with it. He began to get interested in Credding."

"Something?" he said, repeating the detective's last word. "What, exactly, do you mean by that, now?"

"Something to go on with, Mr. Bridgwater," replied Credding with a smile. He tapped the breast of his coat at the place beneath which the little notebook lay. "Got quite a lot of information about the late Mr. Martin Severfield, haven't we? A very wealthy gentleman — no near relations — about to be married to a young and charming lady — and has left her all he had — all! — and named her as sole executor of his last will and testament. Lot in all that, sir."

The banker rubbed his chin, looking from one man to the other.

"I don't like all this!" he said suddenly. "Frankly, I'm surprised about it. As I told you before," he went on, nodding at the detective, "we hold a very large sum of money — an unusually large sum — belonging to Mr. Severfield. He'd been selling out his interests in various affairs and lodging the proceeds with us with a view to reinvestment in England. Naturally, I'm anxious about that, now that he is dead. And — you seem to suggest foul play!"

"Can't say definitely, Mr. Bridgwater," remarked the inspector. "That's more a question for the doctors. They haven't decided — they're going to have a post-mortem."

Bridgwater rose and gave signs of departure.

"Well, I must go back to town," he said. "Of course, I shall come to the inquest. By the by — do either of you know anything of the Mr. Colinrake who was here just now? A London solicitor, of course, but perhaps...?"

The inspector and the detective shook their heads. Credding gave the banker a sly glance.

"I've no doubt you have a solicitor of your own, Mr. Bridgwater?" he remarked quietly. "Of course! Well, one solicitor in London generally knows something about another solicitor in London — or, if he doesn't, he soon can — eh?"

Bridgwater nodded his comprehension and went away — to catch the next express. He spent his hour's journey between Brighton and London in thinking things over, and the more he thought, the more uncomfortable he grew. He remained uncomfortable; he had no appetite for his dinner that evening; the two or three glasses of old port which it was his custom to allow himself failed to restore him to his usual equanimity. But he suddenly remembered, as he slowly sipped the last one, that his solicitor, Arthur Wendover, whom he considered a very smart young fellow, lived, in his private capacity, in a range of flats not far off — to wit, in Cadogan Street — and he finished his wine, got into an overcoat, and went round to find him.

Wendover was at home and alone in his comfortable bachelor flat, and within ten minutes had heard the whole of the banker's story. He was smoking a briar pipe, and he continued to pull at it for a minute or two after Bridgwater had finished talking. Then he knocked out the ashes with great deliberation, put the pipe in a rack on his mantelpiece, and thrusting his hands in the pockets of his trousers, wagged his head solemnly at his elderly client.

"If Severfield's will is properly executed, and is in order otherwise, and if he was of sound mind when it was made," he said, "it'll stand — especially if, as seems to be the case, he had no near relations. A man can leave his money to whom he pleases — as you know."

"I know — I know!" admitted Bridgwater testily. "Of course I know! But you must see for yourself that this is — well, an exceptional case. I might even say a suspicious case; some men wouldn't hesitate about calling it suspicious."

"How — exactly?" asked Wendover.

"How? Good heavens! Look at the facts! Here's a man of middle age, who's worth a big lot of money, gets engaged to be married, suddenly — I'm sure it was sudden — to a girl of twenty — something. He immediately makes a will, leaving her everything he has! And almost as immediately he's found with his neck broken, and an ugly mark on his head which the doctors seem to believe was made before his neck was broken. Murder! Murder! — that's about it!"

"You aren't suggesting that Miss Greville — whoever she may be — murdered Mr. Severfield?"

"Suggesting nothing! I'm only saying — what's it look like?"

"If it were not for the contusion on the temple, I should say it looked like mere coincidence that the engagement, the making of the will, the sudden death, all came, as you might say, close together. What more natural than that a man, passionately in love with a girl, as middle-aged men generally are when there is a girl in the case, should leave his money to her? If everything's in order. Miss Greville will get the money. What's to prevent?"

Bridgwater made no answer, and after a moment's silence, Wendover laughed.

"Besides — what's it matter to you? You aren't in question. And if the man has no relations —"

Bridgwater thrust out his hands with an impatient gesture.

"It's a — a feeling!" he said. "A sort of intuition that there's something wrong. Of course, there's mystery. That woman, now, that certainly was with Severfield in the taxicab? Who was she? Had he gone down to Brighton to meet her? And why hasn't she come forward?"

"Scarcely time for that, I think," remarked Wendover.

"I don't know about that. As far as I could gather, the news had spread pretty well all round Brighton by ten o'clock this morning. There was a special edition of a local paper, with full details and a description supplied by the police, out, and selling in the streets by eleven. If the woman was in Brighton she must have heard. Why — if her meeting and accompanying of Severfield was of an innocent nature — didn't she come forward at once?"

"Big question!" said Wendover, with a smile. He selected another pipe and began to fill it from a jar of tobacco. "I rather gather that you don't know very much about the late Mr. Severfield?" he added. "That so?"

"Well, I don't," admitted the banker. "About his private affairs, anyway. He came to me, on his arrival in England, some eight or nine months ago, with a letter of introduction from customers of ours in Brazil, and began to bank with us, and we became pretty friendly and intimate. But — no, I can't say that I knew anything much of him, privately. This solicitor I mentioned just now, Colinrake, seems to have known more, and he says that Severfield always said he had no near relations."

"I'll tell you what you, as his banker, would be justified in doing," observed Wendover, after a pause, "And, if you like, I'll do it for you. Put an advertisement in *The Times,* at the same time asking the chief provincial, colonial, and foreign newspapers to copy it, stating the bare fact of Severfield's sudden death and requesting anyone who can give information about him, or any relation of his, to come forward. That might produce something."

"Do it!" exclaimed Bridgwater. "Do it at once! As to the colonial and foreign papers copying, you'd better be precise about that. I know where his foreign and colonial interests lay — Australia, South Africa, as regards the colonies: China, India, and Argentine, as regards foreign countries. Also, he had had some concern in a business in New Orleans. Mention these names in your advertisement. Excellent notion of yours — I hadn't thought of it. Get it done — first thing to-morrow. Well, now, there's another thing. Do you know anything of this solicitor, Leicester Colinrake?"

"Nothing!" replied Wendover. "Never heard of him. Where does he hang out — Southampton Street, Strand? Oh — clean out of my beat. But — why?"

"Seeing that he's acted for Severfield, and has Severfield's will, which concerns an estate that, to my knowledge, is one of probably six or seven hundred thousand pounds, it's only likely that I should want to know something about him!" said the banker. "You've never come across him in your professional work?"

"Never — don't know him at all! But," continued Wendover with a sly laugh, "if you want to know all about him, I can soon satisfy your curiosity!"

"How?" demanded Bridgwater.

"You know my clerk, Orridge — the redhaired one?" said Wendover. "The chap who usually shows you in when you call? Very well — Master Orridge, whose age is supposed to be about twenty-five, but whom I confidently believe to be about ninety, has a most unholy and extraordinary knowledge of what we may call the personal or family history of members of my profession in London — I think he's a sort of Paul Pry! Anyway, Orridge is peculiarly learned, in that way, and he'll know all about Colinrake — or soon will know!"

"Find out what you can," said Bridgwater.

"Well, I must go. Oh, one thing more. I shall, of course, attend the inquest at Brighton and you must go with me. Now supposing it turns out to be a case of murder —"

"I never suppose anything!" interrupted Wendover. "Wait!"

Chapter V
Miss Beatrix Greville

Bridgwater waited — and had no further news of anything until late the next afternoon, when Credding telephoned to him. The inquest, said Credding, had been fixed for ten o'clock on the following morning; he hoped Bridgwater would be there in good time, for he believed there would be unexpected developments. And at the hour specified the banker was there, and Wendover with him; Credding met them at the door of the coroner's court and drew him aside.

"Those developments you mentioned?" asked Bridgwater, after introducing Wendover as his solicitor. "What are they?"

"Well — the thing's developed a bit in two directions," replied the detective. "One is that the doctors — three of 'em — are convinced that that wound on the temple was caused by a heavy blow from some blunt instrument before death, though they think it didn't cause death. They're of opinion that Severfield was struck down, rendered unconscious, and then thrown over the cliff. That's — murder! What the motive may have been, seeing that Severfield had plenty of money on him, and a good deal of valuable property in the way of personal adornments, and that it was all untouched, we don't know — it wasn't robbery!"

"Well — and what else?" asked Bridgwater.

"This. Of course we discussed the matter thoroughly with the coroner," continued Credding." And in view of the fact that Colinrake told us of Severfield's engagement to this Miss Greville, and of Simpson's statement about the lady in furs who got into his cab with Severfield, the coroner decided to summon Miss Greville as a witness. She was served with the summons yesterday, at her flat in London, and she's here — just gone into the court with Colinrake. I don't think Colinrake likes it — all the same, the coroner's officer, who had to go to him for the young lady's address, had no opposition from him."

"But what can she tell?" asked Bridgwater. "Colinrake, I think, said he'd seen her in London at the time that Severfield was here in Brighton. She couldn't possibly be the lady spoken of by Simpson!"

"No — but she may know who that lady was," replied Credding. "Severfield, as he was engaged to her, may have told her why he came to Brighton. Anyway, it'll be interesting to hear her examined. We — the police, I mean — have a pretty sharp man watching the case; we're not leaving any stone unturned, Mr. Bridgwater, for we're confident it is murder. And a particularly brutal murder, too!"

"You — yourself?" asked Wendover. "Have you found out anything new?"

Credding glanced at his watch.

"It's time we were inside," he said. "You'll hear everything I know pretty soon — I shall be called. Come this way — I've kept seats for you."

The two men, following the detective to a table in the centre of the crowded court, found themselves placed near the man and woman of whom they had just been talking. They inspected Miss Greville with a good deal of curiosity — a tall, handsome young woman, dark-eyed, dark-haired, whose colouring suggested some nationality other than English; Italian, thought Wendover. She had already assumed mourning garments, and wore a veil, but it seemed to these keen-eyed watchers that there were no traces of undue grief on her distinctly pretty face, and that she regarded the proceedings with complete composure. Nor were there any signs of less composure evident in her companion; Colinrake, alert and watchful though he was, appeared to view the inquiry as a matter of course.

There was little at first of which Bridgwater and Wendover were not already aware. Colinrake identified the body, and said what he knew of the dead man; Bridgwater found himself unexpectedly asked to prove that Severfield was a man of great wealth. Hopperson told his story; Credding told his, with the addition that he had traced a good deal of Severfield's movements on the afternoon of his arrival in Brighton between half-past three and six o'clock and that he had been always alone. Simpson told his story of the ride in the taxicab, and of the lady in furs; a police inspector testified that so far that lady had not come forward, nor had the police been able to come across the least trace of her. Then came the medical witnesses — they agreed, as a result of their investigations, that Severfield, in all probability, had been struck down and rendered insensible by a blow on the head, and had then been thrown over the cliff, thereby receiving injuries which resulted in immediate death. So far, there was nothing sensational, and little that had not been anticipated by the better-informed spectators; the interest deepened when the dead man's fiancee was shown into the witness-box, to be gently questioned by the coroner. Undoubtedly attractive, decided Bridgwater, as she raised her veil; undoubtedly un-English, again thought Wendover, less sentimental. Still, Greville is, or has long become, an English name, and Miss Greville owned to an English domicile in Madresfield Mansions, Bloomsbury, and her accent quickly proved that she had learnt her (presumably) mother-tongue in London.

"I understand that you were engaged to be married to the unfortunate gentleman, Mr. Martin Severfield, into the circumstances of whose death we are inquiring?" suggested the coroner sympathetically and in tones which implied that he would trouble the witness as little as possible. "Just so — just so. Now, you have heard. Miss Greville, that Mr. Severfield was seen here in Brighton just after eight o'clock on Monday evening last, in company with a lady who" — here the coroner glanced at an expensive fur cloak which the witness had discarded on entering the box — "who, in fact, wore furs. Will you kindly tell us if you were that lady?"

"Oh, no! I was not in Brighton — I was in London — at home — that night."

"Did you know that Mr. Severfield was visiting Brighton?"

"Oh, yes. He told me of it."

"When did he tell you?"

"On Monday morning, before he left London. He called to see me, and said he was going to Brighton that afternoon for a day or two."

"Did he give you any reason — say why he was going?"

"No — none!"

"Did he speak of having any appointment with anyone here?"

"No. He just said he was going."

"Has Mr. Severfield ever said anything to you which would make you think that he had enemies — that he was in danger of his life?"

"Oh, no — never!"

"From your knowledge of him, you don't know of any reason why anyone should attack him — should want to take his life?"

"Oh, no! I know of nothing of that sort."

The coroner paused — hesitated — evidently decided that he had no more to ask. He murmured some polite words of condolence, and intimated that Miss Greville might stand down. But before Miss Greville could turn to leave the witness-box, the keen-faced man-of-law who represented the police was on his feet.

"With your permission, sir, I wish to put certain questions to this witness," he said. "They are comparatively few in number, but they are of importance, considering the grave aspect which this matter has assumed." He turned to the witness. "How long had you been engaged to be married to the late Mr. Severfield at the time of his death?" he asked.

Wendover, watching closely, saw the slightest exchange of glances between Miss Greville and Colinrake. But it was so slight that there was no noticeable delay in her reply.

"About three weeks."

"Quite recently! How long had you known Mr. Severfield when the engagement took place?"

"Oh — a few months."

"How many months?"

"Eight — or nine — I think."

"Then he must have met you very soon after his arrival in England?"

"Yes — soon after."

"Where did Mr. Severfield meet you — first?"

Again the interchange of glances — and this time not so ready a reply.

"Well, it was at Mr. Colinrake's office."

"Where Mr. Severfield, I suppose, had gone on business. Had you, too, gone there on business?"

"No. I — I was engaged there."

"In what capacity?"

38

"I was Mr. Colinrake's secretary."

"How long had you been Mr. Colinrake's secretary?"

"About — two years, I think."

"Had you been engaged in a similar capacity previously?"

"Not exactly — I'd learned shorthand and typewriting."

"I see! Well — and Mr. Severfield, after meeting you at Mr. Colinrake's, fell in love with you? At once?"

"I — I suppose so. He said so."

"Began to pay court to you, anyway. How soon did he ask you to marry him?"

"Well — when we became engaged."

"About three weeks ago, eh? And in the meantime — between your first meeting him at Mr. Colinrake's office and the date of the engagement — I suppose he had shown you a great deal of attention?"

"Yes!"

"What form, or forms, did that take?"

"I don't understand you!"

"Well, did he take you out — to the theatre — to dinner — did he give you presents — make himself agreeable to you?"

"Oh, yes — all that!"

"Played the part of a suitor, generally, eh, until it finally culminated in a definite offer of marriage — which you at once accepted?"

"Yes — I think so."

"Had all that gone on from the very first?"

"He was very attentive — from the very first."

"A case of love at first sight! Very well — where do you live. Miss Greville?"

"83, Madresfield Mansions, Bloomsbury."

"Flat?"

"Yes."

"Alone?"

"No! My aunt lives with me. And two servants."

"Quite an establishment! Those are very select and superior flats, I believe — and the rents are high, aren't they? How long have you lived in yours?"

"Since — since June."

"Five months. Where did you live before that?"

"In Bernard Street."

"Lodgings?"

"Yes."

"Was your aunt with you in Bernard Street?"

"No. She came when we took the flat in Madresfield Mansions."

"When who took the flat?"

"Well, she and I took it."

"Were you paid a big salary at Mr. Colinrake's?"

"No — only a proper one."

"I'm afraid I must ask you how much?"

"It was three guineas a week."

"And the rent of the flat at Madresfield Mansions is — what?"

"I — I believe it's six hundred a year."

"Don't you know, definitely? Didn't you — and your aunt — pay the rent?"

"No. Mr. Severfield paid it."

"Oh! — Mr. Severfield paid it, did he? From — the beginning?"

"From the time we went in."

"How came Mr. Severfield — to whom you were not engaged in June, you know — to set you and your aunt in this expensive flat? Say, please!"

"We — we were gradually becoming engaged. He didn't like my living in lodgings in Bernard Street, and he persuaded me to let him take the flat for me, and to get my aunt to come and live with me. Of course, I — I knew we should become engaged."

"I see — you had an intuition! So that from last June right up to the time of his death, Mr. Severfield was paying the rent of your flat — and, I suppose, all the expenses connected with its upkeep — servants and everything? Gave you a cheque every week, eh?"

"No — he gave it to my aunt."

"What is your aunt's name. Miss Greville?"

"Miss Brown — Miss Henrietta Brown."

"Is she here?"

Colinrake, who had been showing signs of restlessness, rose to his feet, looking at the coroner.

"Miss Brown can be here within three hours, sir," he said. "This examination is taking —"

"This examination will take whatever turn I choose to give it!" said the sharp-faced man. He waved Colinrake aside, and turned to his witness. "Father's sister?" he inquired.

"My mother's sister."

"We will have Miss Brown later on. Now, Miss Greville — another question. Did Mr. Severfield ever tell you that he had made a will in your favour?"

"No! But when we arranged to marry he said that he should provide handsomely for me."

"Do you know that he has made a will in your favour?"

"I do now."

"Since when?"

"Since the day after his death. Mr. Colinrake told me."

"And did Mr. Colinrake tell you the provisions?"

"Yes," replied Miss Greville, composedly. "Mr. Severfield has left me his entire fortune!"

Chapter VI
Orridge

There was something so frank, so absolutely ingenuous in the witness's answer that the eager listeners could not refrain from laughing; even the coroner, who had been Closely watching the proceedings with an evident growing suspicion that there was more behind all this than was apparent, relaxed into a smile. Before the ripple of laughter died away, Colinrake was on his feet.

"I appeal to you, sir, as solicitor for the late Mr. Severfield, and also as representing this witness, that you should now adjourn these proceedings," he said. "My friend here has throughout treated Miss Greville, who is here under very sad circumstances, as if — as if — I really don't know how to phrase what I feel about it! — except that I feel very indignant. He has introduced an element of — well, to say the least, suspicion, into the case — and, I think, in an unwarrantable fashion. I ask you, sir, to adjourn, in order that I may bring proof of the absolute propriety of my late client's relations with Miss Greville, and, in particular, to have an opportunity of bringing her aunt, Miss Brown, here, who can say —"

"I am not aware," interrupted the police advocate, rising, "that I have made any reflections on the propriety or the impropriety of whatever relations existed' between this witness and Mr. Severfield. I have established certain facts which show that Mr. Severfield met this young lady at Mr. Colinrake's office, that after a very short time he provided her with an expensive establishment, and that not long before his death he made a will in which, as she candidly says, he bequeathed all he had to her. Now, according to the medical and other evidence, Mr. Severfield was undoubtedly murdered, and we naturally want to know all we can, and by every available means —"

"I think this would be a convenient stage of the proceedings at which to adjourn," broke in the coroner. "Shall we say for a fortnight from to-day? In the meantime, gentlemen," he went on, turning to the jury, "you will..."

Bridgwater and Wendover, leaving the coroner warning the jurymen not to let their minds be influenced by anything they might hear or read before their reassembling, left the court, followed by Credding. The detective seemed highly diverted.

"That was ten minutes of the best, eh, gentlemen?" he said, rubbing his hands. "Now, is that girl a highly accomplished actress, or is she what they term an — an — what is it? — I'm not good at French."

"*Ingenue,*" suggested Wendover.

"That's it, sir — the very word! Which? Her last answer was — artless in the last degree! Artless — just that! But — was it assumed? Anyway," continued Credding, "that bit of examination by our man — clever fellow, isr.'t he? — is helpful. You know, gentlemen, it looks very fishy! Severfield executes a will, leaving this young woman all he had — a huge fortune — and almost immediately afterwards he's found murdered! Very, very fishy!"

"You're not suggesting that she murdered him?" said Wendover cynically.

"Oh, dear me, no, sir, not I!" replied Credding." But it might be in the interest of somebody to knock Severfield on the head so that she could get the money! However, we're only at the beginning. Of course, now that we've made a start, everything about the late Mr. Severfield, including his proposed marriage, will have to be thoroughly investigated. By the by, I saw that advertisement you've put in *The Times,* Mr. Wendover, on behalf of Mr. Bridgwater's banking firm. Now, if you get any information from anybody, you'll let us know, won't you? This is like one of those puzzles that the youngsters play with, sir — those things in which there are a hundred little pieces. Fit 'em together, piece by piece, and — but you know what I mean. The merest tiniest scrap of information! — eh?"

Wendover promised that if he received any news he would communicate it to the Brighton police, and he and Bridgwater went away and returned to London. The banker hurried off to report the morning's doings to his partners. Wendover repaired to his office, and after going through his correspondence with his managing clerk, bade him send in the man he had mentioned to Bridgwater when the banker called on him at his flat — Orridge.

Orridge came hurrying in — a sharp-faced, red-haired, alert little fellow, who looked as if he were perpetually hungering and thirsting for something to do; he suggested a lively terrier, keen on possible rats, and when he entered his restless eyes fixed themselves on his employer with a questioning as eloquent as words. Wendover laughed.

"Oh, yes, a job after your own heart, Orridge!" he said, as if in answer. "Sit down."

Orridge perched himself on the edge of a chair and rubbed his knees with a pair of long, thin, bony hands; his gestures betokened his desire to get at something.

"Look here, Orridge," began Wendover. "This is between ourselves. Do you know a solicitor named Leicester Colinrake?"

"Mr. Leicester Colinrake, Southampton Street, Strand," snapped out Orridge. "Yes, sir!"

"What do you know about him?"

"Know he is a solicitor. Been in practice, I should say, about eleven or twelve years. Know him by sight. Spoken to him now and then. Attended his office once or twice, before I came to you. Oh, yes, I know Mr. Leicester Colinrake!"

"What sort of practice has he, Orridge?"

"Middling! Bit of county court work. Bit of police court work. That sort of thing, chiefly. General — as you might say. No great amount. Keeps on going — comfortably."

"Not a big establishment, eh?" suggested Wendover.

"Couple of clerks and an office-boy," replied Orridge. "That's about it."

"Have you ever heard, or do you know of his having a lady secretary?"

Orridge grinned, showing a double row of pointed teeth. When he grinned like that, thought Wendover, he resembled a rat-hunting terrier more than ever.

"Miss Greville!" chuckled Orridge. "Oh, yes — I know Miss Greville!"

"The devil you do!" exclaimed Wendover, under his breath. "Um! What do you know about Miss Greville?" he added aloud.

"As you say — Colinrake's secretary. Good-looking young woman — smart appearance — dresses herself up to the mark! Been there some time. Miss Greville has — a couple of years, I should say. Seen her about with Colinrake, too. Very thick, they are. Judging from appearances."

"Where have you seen them about — together?"

"Theatres — music-halls — restaurants. Seen 'em together, too, in the Bloomsbury district. I live there, you know, Mr. Wendover — Marchmont Street. Miss Greville, she used to live in Bernard Street. Haven't seen her about there, though, for some little time now."

"And you've seen Colinrake with her there — in that district?"

"Frequently! Of an evening — as if they were going out to dinner together — that sort of thing. Oh, yes — I know 'em both well enough, Mr. Wendover! By sight."

Wendover digested this information during a brief silence. He was beginning to think something, but he was not quite sure what — everything was vague. He turned suddenly on his clerk.

"You know a lot of solicitors' clerks, don't you, Orridge?" he suggested." And no doubt you hear a good deal of talk — gossip?"

"No end!" assented Orridge, with a chuckle. "Heaps!"

"Ever hear anything about Colinrake and Miss Greville?"

"Yes! Heard some chaps say they were engaged. Heard others suggest they were married. Can't say myself, of course — don't know enough."

"Well, I want you to know more," said Wendover. "Listen to me." He proceeded to give Orridge, a keenly attentive listener, a full and particular account of all that had taken place at the inquest that morning, laying special stress on Miss Greville's evidence. "Now," he concluded, "I want you to find out all you can about Miss Greville. You know how to do it better than I can suggest to you. Use your own methods. Drop whatever work you're doing in the office now, and take a few days off. Ask Mr. Johnston to give you whatever money you want for expenses. And as soon as you've anything to tell, come and tell it. You understand?"

"I understand," replied Orridge. He rose, buttoned his coat, as if to prepare for immediate action, and turned to the door. But before he reached it, he turned back, glancing speculatively at Wendover. "So that's how it stands, is it?" he asked. "Everything is left to this young woman?"

"According to Colinrake — yes," replied Wendover. "Everything!"

"And Colinrake drew the will, and has it?" inquired Orridge.

"Yes — so I understand," said Wendover. "Why?"

"Colinrake, Mr. Wendover," said Orridge, "is a very sharp, astute man! I've known of one or two queerish cases in which he manifested those qualities. I think you'll find, as regards this will, that if this man Severfield was, as he appears to have been, in his right mind when he made it, it'll stand! But then, of course, you haven't said that anyone wants to contest it."

"I haven't," replied Wendover. "I don't know of anyone who's in a position to contest it. What I want to know is precisely what I've asked you to find out."

"Precisely!" assented Orridge. He still lingered, and Wendover, glancing at him, fancied that the terrier-like expression had been transformed into one of thoughtful reflection. "There's another thing, Mr. Wendover," he remarked suddenly. "It may have a bearing on this matter. I think you should get to know, if you can, how Colinrake stands — financially."

"If possible, yes," agreed Wendover.

"I can do it," said Orridge. "You can leave it to me. I've an idea — basis for it, of course — that Colinrake's a bit of a gambler!"

"Ah!" exclaimed Wendover. something of that?"

"Something. I'll know more. Well —"

He suddenly nodded abruptly, and left the room, and Wendover turned to his telephone and ringing up Bridgwater, asked him to come round. Bridgwater came — and listened intently to Wendover's account of his conversation with Orridge.

"It comes to this," concluded Wendover. "Severfield has left all his money to a young woman who has been mixed up with Colinrake for some time, and it looks to me as if she'd get it, unless —"

"Unless — what?" asked Bridgwater.

"Unless it could be proved that a conspiracy to get rid of Severfield existed, in which Colinrake and this young woman had some share," replied Wendover slowly. "An ugly thing to think of, but —"

"You mean — a conspiracy to murder Severfield?"

"Well — bad as it sounds — yes. I suppose that's what I do mean. There's no doubt of the fact that the affair does look — what that chap Credding called it this morning — fishy! Very! Here's a man makes a will, leaving everything to one person, and almost immediately afterwards he's murdered! Come!"

"I shouldn't think that the young woman was a party to any conspiracy of that sort," said Bridgwater after a pause.

"The young woman may be an absolute cat's-paw!" said Wendover. "As innocent of all offence as ever they make 'em. Perhaps she is — I shouldn't wonder if she is, from what one saw of her. But — what's behind?"

"Colinrake!" said the banker.

"Well, maybe. And, maybe, there are others. We don't know," replied Wendover. "What's certain is that Severfield was murdered. Why?"

"That's for the police to find out," said Bridgwater. "Their affair — chiefly."

"It's for anybody and everybody who's concerned to find out!" retorted Wendover. "I wish we knew more about Severfield," he went on. "Don't you know more than you've told me? Did he never mention people to you?"

"I don't think he knew any people — here," replied Bridgwater. "He no doubt knew a few booksellers, and picture dealers, and that sort — I told you he was a bit of a collector — but I question if he knew people in private life."

"Well, he evidently knew the woman he met at Brighton," said Wendover.

"Don't see that!" asserted the banker. "She may have been a mere chance acquaintance. If she'd been a friend of his, she'd have come forward. It strikes me, you know, that Severfield may have been lured to that spot where he was killed, or to somewhere about there. What was he doing there, anyway? I wish the police would find that woman!"

"I think Severfield knew her," said Wendover. "I think he had an appointment with her. Remember this — he walked out of the Grand International Hotel shortly after eight o'clock; within a few minutes he was in company with this woman and stepping into Simpson's taxicab with her, with a request to be driven to the end of Ovingdean Lane. Don't those facts suggest a meeting by appointment? It was probably to keep that appointment that Severfield went to Brighton."

"I know Ovingdean well enough," observed the banker. "I know all that coast. Ovingdean is a very small village — the police could have combed it out in an hour or two; I wonder if they have? Because it was at the end of the lane leading to Ovingdean that Simpson last saw these two."

"Yes — but Simpson didn't see them go up the lane!" said Wendover. "Simpson left them talking at the roadside. And I, too, know that coast, and, as you'll probably remember, there are a good many newly-built houses, bungalows, and so on about that particular stretch, as you go towards Rottingdean. Was Severfield inveigled into one of those houses —"

Before he could say more, Wendover was interrupted by the entrance of Johnston, the managing clerk, who handed him a card.

"Elderly gentleman — in the waiting-room, sir," he said as if in explanation. "He wishes to see you in reference to the advertisement in this morning's *Times* — case of the late Mr. Severfield, sir."

Chapter VII
The Australian Sheep Station

Wendover glanced sharply at the card and read out what he saw there: "Mr. Henry Marsland, 53, Collingham Road, Bedford — show Mr. Marsland in at once, Johnston," he proceeded. Then he turned to Bridgwater. "Quick work, eh?" he said. "But I believed it would have quick effect, that advertisement — I felt sure there'd be somebody who knew, or who knew something about Severfield. Well —"

Mr. Marsland was entering — a tall, grey-haired, grey-bearded man whose face looked as if it had been browned by tropic suns and weather-beaten by tropic winds. He glanced interrogatively from one man to the other.

"Mr. Wendover?" he inquired.

The solicitor rose, bowed, drew forward a chair, and waved a hand toward the banker.

"I'm Mr. Wendover, Mr. Marsland," he answered. "Take a seat. This is Mr. Bridgwater, head of the banking firm on whose behalf I inserted the advertisement in this morning's *Times,* about which, I understand, you wish to see me? You can tell us something about the late Mr. Severfield, eh?"

"I think so," replied the visitor. He took the chair which Wendover had placed for him, and unbuttoning his overcoat, slowly drew off his gloves, meanwhile making a deliberate and careful inspection of the other two men. "Yes, I think so, Mr. Wendover — I think so! I have seen the portrait of Severfield which the police have supplied to the papers, and I've no doubt whatever that he is the Martin Severfield I knew, and knew very well, some twenty year ago."

"Good!" exclaimed Wendover. "And — where did you know him?"

"In Australia. He had a sheep-station next to my own, in the Gooloogong district."

"What part of Australia is that, Mr. Marsland?"

"About two hundred miles due west of Sydney — New South Wales. I had been on my station two or three years when

Severfield came to his. It will be, as near as I can reckon, twenty or twenty-one years since he took up his station, and he was on it about two years. I got to know him pretty soon after his arrival, and I saw him frequently during his stay. Our stations were not quite as far apart as is often the case out there — twelve or fifteen miles, in our case. So — relatively — we were close to each other."

"How old would Severfield be at that time?"

"He was over thirty. I should say, thirty-two or -three. I remember him well enough — a reserved sort of man, spare of speech — some people would have called him morose. He and I got on very well, though. But we were scarcely close friends — neighbours, friendly neighbours, you know."

"Did he ever tell you much about himself?"

"Nothing! I gathered that he was a man of means, though — by no means dependent on his success as a sheep-farmer. No — he never told me anything of his private affairs before coming to his station. But — I learned a good deal about them, later on! That is, about affairs that took place there."

"Domestic affairs?"

"Domestic affairs, certainly! And of a very curious, even queer nature, in my opinion. I read something in the papers yesterday and again this morning about Severfield's death at Brighton, and I've been wondering since if what took place out there in New South Wales had any relation to what's happened here — I mean, whether, if Severfield was murdered the other night, which seems highly probable, the murder has arisen out of the strange circumstances of twenty years ago?"

"I don't think there's any doubt that Severfield was murdered, Mr. Marsland," said Wendover. "Mr. Bridgwater and myself have only just returned from attending the opening of the inquest at Brighton this morning, and the medical evidence points to the conclusion that he was murdered — undoubtedly! But — what were the strange circumstances you refer to?"

"I'll tell you," replied Marsland. "That, of course, is what I came to town for — I think, considering what has happened, they should be known. Severfield, when he came to his sheep-station, adjacent to mine, was a single man. What's more, he was the sort of man that you'd expect to remain single — not a lady's man at all: he didn't appear to have the least interest in women.

Well, when he'd been my neighbour for about fifteen months, Severfield went to Sydney — on business. He was away from his sheep-station some five or six weeks. Then he returned, bringing with him two young ladies — both little more than girls — I should say they were both under twenty. I happened to come across the party on their way from the railway to Severfield's place, and he introduced one of the young ladies — the younger one, whom I set down as a girl of eighteen — as his wife; the other as her sister. I was, of course, immensely surprised, though I took care not to show it — Severfield, I knew, was a very sensitive man. He asked me to call and see them; and, of course, I went — went fairly often."

"Were you also a bachelor at that time?" asked Wendover.

"I was. But I was engaged to a lady in Melbourne, whom I afterwards — a year or so afterwards — married. So — if that's what you're thinking of — Mrs. Severfield's sister didn't appeal! In fact, neither of the two young ladies appealed to me. They were both very pretty — very! But I saw from the first moment I set eyes on them that they were absolutely unfitted for life on an Australian sheep-station — it was like putting a couple of hot-house flowers in the middle of a potato-patch! They were essentially town girls — used, I should say, to a life of excitement and pleasure. Of course, I knew nothing about him, and I didn't learn anything — Severfield never said a word to me. But from what I saw, and from chance remarks, I came to the conclusion that both girls had been on the stage — probably as dancers."

"Did you ever — later on, I mean — ascertain that?" asked Wendover. "Ever get any particulars?"

"No! I never heard anything of their antecedents," replied Marsland. "Severfield, as I said just now, told me nothing. I concluded, of course, that he'd met these young ladies at Sydney. But he may have met them elsewhere — he'd been away long enough to have been down to Melbourne. Again, they might have come out to him, from England. His real reason for going away might have been to meet them on their arrival at Melbourne or Sydney. I knew nothing, you see."

"But you'd hear some names?" suggested Wendover.

"The sister was introduced to me as Miss May," answered Marsland. "I don't know what her Christian name was. The two girls called each other by what I took to be nicknames — pet names: Severfield always addressed them by those names. Mrs. Severfield was known as Pip; Miss May was Pop."

"Playful!" remarked Wendover. "Well, Mr. Marsland — and how did things go?"

"You must remember that I wasn't absolutely next door," said Marsland. "I only went over to Severfield's place now and then. At first, I should say, things went all right — the novelty of their new life and surroundings no doubt appealed to the young ladies. But happening to go there one time a bit later on, it struck me that they were both beginning to be a bit bored. You can't wonder! — there was no society, no gaiety, nothing to interest a couple of young girls. Still, I wasn't prepared for the sudden smash-up!"

"Smash-up, eh?" said Wendover. "And — what form did that take?"

"Severfield, about six months after his bringing these girls back, went off one day to inspect an outlying portion of his station," continued Marsland. "His station was four or five times the size of mine — it extended a long way to the north and northwest. He was away three of four days. When he came back, his wife and her sister had disappeared — clean gone! It turned out, when he made inquiry of the folk at his house, that within a few hours of his leaving they'd set off for the nearest railway station, saying that they were going to do some shopping at Bathurst, and would return in a day or two. But they didn't return — and Severfield couldn't get any news of them. And, presently, he went in search of them — and that was the last that was seen of him in those parts!"

"Never came back?" exclaimed Wendover.

"Never came back!" assented Marsland. "Now, I never saw him, or the two girls, about that time — hadn't seen any one of the three for some weeks: I only got to hear of this affair — the news, of course, spread quickly — after Severfield had gone. Very soon, another queer thing happened. Three days after Severfield had set off in search of his runaways, a stranger — described to me as a good-looking young Englishman who appeared to be in a very ugly mood — rode up to Severfield's sheep-station and wanted to see Mrs. Severfield. Hearing what had taken place, he made some inquiries, and went off. Who he was, nobody knew, and anyway, he never came back. Nor did Mrs. Severfield return; nor her sister — nor Severfield himself."

"Did you ever hear of them?" asked Wendover.

"Of the two girls, nothing," answered Marsland. "Never heard one word about them from then to the time I left Australia, six or seven years ago. But those of us in the neighbourhood heard of Severfield. About two months after he'd gone in search of his wife, a couple of men came to his sheep-station. One was a lawyer; the other a man to whom Severfield had sold the whole place and everything on it. The lawyer had the papers — he'd come with the new owner to put him in possession. And after that I never heard of Severfield again until yesterday."

The three men looked at each other, in turn, and for a few moments each seemed to be engaged in his own thoughts. Bridgwater broke the silence.

"That young man who rode up making inquiries, Mr. Marsland?" he said. "Do I understand that he asked for Mrs. Severfield?"

"So I was told by the people at Severfield's house. Then — for her sister. He was evidently in search of, or wanted to see, the two young women."

"Did you hear his name?"

"No — as far as I'm aware, he never gave his name. The man who told me of the occurrence said that when this young fellow had learned what had happened — that Mrs. Severfield and her sister had disappeared, and that Severfield had set off to find them — he went off muttering, with a face as black as thunder."

"Interesting!" said Wendover. "Very interesting. And — it's twenty years ago!"

"Precisely!" assented Marsland. "It is! — twenty years ago. Still — "

Bridgwater interrupted him. The banker was evidently thinking of how this information could be turned to account.

"Can you tell us, Mr. Marsland," he asked, "what bank Severfield did business with when he was your neighbour in Australia?"

"Yes!" replied Marsland promptly. "Certainly! The same bank that I had my account with. The Bank of New South Wales

— head office, Sydney; and branches all over that part of the country."

"Thank you," said Bridgwater. "We might find out something about Severfield's movements, after going in search of his wife, through the bank," he added, turning to Wendover. "He'd want money, and he probably had further transactions. And twenty years, after all, is not such a very great stretch of time."

"The thing is — how does this information bear on recent events?" remarked Wendover. "You know, for instance, from what he told you that during the last twenty years, Severfield has had business dealings in more than one country. Evidently, after selling his property in Australia, he became something of a rolling stone. That looks as if he never found his wife. Now, I'm wondering if she's alive? I'm wondering, too, if, when it gets out in the papers that Severfield's left some six or seven hundred thousand pounds, it mayn't bring her forward — if she is alive!"

"What could she do — if she did come forward?" asked Bridgwater.

"Um! — problematical — can't say, off-hand," replied Wendover. "By the by," he added, suddenly turning to Marsland. "I suppose, as your memory seems to be a remarkably good one, that you can describe the two sisters? What were they like?"

"I can describe them as they were when I knew them — twenty years ago!" said Marsland. "As I told you at first, I should say that they were then both under twenty. I took the sister, known to me as Miss May, to be nineteen — Mrs. Severfield to be about a year younger. They were handsome young women, with very good figures, lithe, lissom — fair-haired, grey-eyed, typical English complexions —"

"They were English?" asked Wendover.

"Oh, undoubtedly English!"

"Of what class?"

"Difficult to say. They spoke quite correctly — pretty voices. I should say they were of quite a good, presentable class."

"And, I suppose, noticeable girls?" suggested Wendover. "It's odd that they should completely disappear! Did you never see anything in the papers about them, or Severfield? — after they'd all cleared out? But of course, you didn't — you've already said you never heard of them again."

"That is so — I never heard of them again — never saw anything in the papers. I formed my own conclusion — which was that the two girls ran away to England, and that Severfield followed them."

Wendover turned to Bridgwater.

"I say, you know!" he exclaimed. "There's a matter of importance that we've forgotten! Severfield's papers ought to be examined. There must be papers at his suite at the hotel. But I suppose Colinrake — "

At that moment Johnston entered with a telegram, and Wendover, with a muttered apology, tore it open, and glanced at the signature first.

"Hallo!" he said. "This is from the detective chap — Credding!"

Chapter VIII
The Roadside Bungalow

After a glance at its contents Wendover handed over the telegram to Bridgwater.

"You see what he says?" he remarked, as he reached across his desk for a railway guide. "Got some fresh information since we saw him this morning, and wants us to go down and hear about it. What do you say?"

"I suppose one must," answered the banker. "Twice in one day — rather tiring work! But it's no doubt important — what about a train?"

"There's one from London Bridge in twenty minutes — express," replied Wendover. "That'll get us to Brighton by five o'clock. After all, when one's on even the faintest trail..."

He hurried Bridgwater off to the station; an hour and ten minutes later he hurried him into the police head-quarters at Brighton in search of Credding. Credding was there, and showed no surprise at the speedy response to his summons.

"Thought you'd come, gentlemen," he said, as he showed them into the room where their previous conversations had taken place. "Well, since I saw you at noon, I've had some information that no doubt bears on this case. From two different men — one a labourer, who lives near Black Rock; the other a bus-conductor on the Brighton-Newhaven route. These men have been here, and their statements have been taken down in writing, read over to them, and signed by them — here they are," he continued, producing two sheets of blue foolscap, "and, if you'll sit down, I'll read them to you. I don't know what you'll say, but I think they're highly important — highly! They fit in with other things."

He took a seat opposite his visitors' chairs, and, unfolding the uppermost of his documents, proceeded to read slowly and carefully, as if he wanted his hearers to take in the full significance of what he read:

My name is David Wright. I am a general labourer, living at Number 6, Columbine Terrace, Kemp Town. I have lived there for many years and know the district very well. On Monday night last, October 16th, I had occasion to go to Rottingdean. I left Rottingdean, to walk home, by way of the high road, about twenty-five minutes to nine o'clock. I walked along leisurely. About half a mile on the east side of Black Rock there is, on the roadside, on the edge of some ground that stretcher from the south side of the road to the edge of the cliffs, a bungalow called Elvescot. It was built two or three years ago. I am not aware who the owner is. There is a placard in the window, but the bungalow stands back about eighty to a hundred yards from the road, and I have never been close to it. I know, however, that it has been empty for some little time. I have noticed that, going to and from my work along that road. On Monday night, as I got near it, I noticed a light in one of the windows. I had noticed earlier in the day that the place was still unlet, so I concluded somebody had come to it that afternoon. It is a furnished bungalow. There are blinds and curtains in all the windows. I did not see any shadows on the blinds. I saw the light move from one window to another, as if somebody was carrying a lamp or a candle about the place. I thought nothing of it, and walked on. It would be all about ten minutes past nine when I saw this light.

(Signed) David Wright.

"That's one, gentlemen," said Credding, laying the document aside, and picking up the other. "Now I may as well tell you, before going further, that the bungalow David Wright refers to is in the same stretch, of ground in which that V-shaped gap in the cliff is, at the foot of which Severfield's body was found. As a matter of fact, it's in a dead straight line above that gap, and from the edge of the gap to the garden in which the bungalow stands the distance is less than two hundred and fifty yards. That's an important detail! But now for the other man's statement." He opened the second paper, and read on in the same leisurely fashion:

My name is Herbert Brownson. I am an omnibus conductor in the service of the Southdown Motor Company. My usual route is from Brighton through Rottingdean to Newhaven, and vice versa. On Monday evening last I was in charge of the bus which is timed to leave Newhaven at nine o'clock. We were a few minutes late in starting that night — about five minutes late. We arrived at Rottingdean about half-past nine. Only one passenger got in there. That was a lady, very smartly dressed in furs — a very smart lady altogether. I should say she was about forty years of age, as near as I could reckon. I noticed her particularly, as she sat near the door, by which I was standing. I could not see her face very well, as she had on a thick veil, and the collar of her fur coat was turned up, but I think she was a very good-looking woman, fresh complexion, and bright hair — what they call golden hair. She had a bag on her knee which I particularly noticed — one of those small bags that ladies carry. It was of bright green leather — morocco leather, in my opinion — ornamented with figures of dragons, or something of that sort, in gilt, and it had gold mountings, and a gold chain which went round the lady's wrist. She took her purse out of this bag when she paid me for her ticket. When we reached Brighton, she left the bus, and I saw her go in the direction of Castle Square and North Street. That would be just about ten o'clock. I could recognise this lady if I saw her again.

(Signed) Herbert Brownson.

Credding folded his documents and put them safely away. The expression of his eyes and lips showed Wendover that he was highly satisfied with the revelations made in them.

"You attach a lot of importance to those pieces of information, don't you, Credding?" he said. "You think you'll get something out of them?"

"Well, they are important, Mr. Wendover," replied the detective cheerily. "At any rate I consider 'em so! The first establishes the fact that somebody was in that bungalow that night about the time that Severfield was around there. The second shows us that it's not going to be such a difficult job after all to trace the mysterious lady. That curious bag of hers will help! But I don't think she'll be found here in Brighton. She probably left Brighton that night. Brownson says he watched her go towards Castle Square and North Street — she was most likely on her way to the station — there's a fast train to Victoria at ten-twenty which she'd just have time to catch. But now, gentlemen, if you'll be so good as to come with me, we'll just get into a taxi-cab and take a little jaunt as far as that bungalow — Elvescot."

Dark had fallen by this time, and the bungalow, set in a recently laid-out garden on the edge of ground sloping towards the cliffs, looked uninviting and chilly. But Credding paid no attention to anything but his business — which was to hasten up to and read, by the light of a lantern which he suddenly produced from an inner pocket, the placard spoken of by the man David Wright.

"Here we are!" he said, waving his lantern along the printed lines. " 'This highly desirable furnished bungalow to let. To view, apply for key at Mr. Fowler's cottage, close by, on the right.' Very good," added Credding, looking round and indicating some cottages a little way down the road. "Now if you gentlemen will stay here, I'll just slip along in search of the key — and of Mr. Fowler."

Left alone, the banker and the solicitor wandered round to the other side of the bungalow. There the sea faced them; they heard the waves washing on the shingle three hundred yards away; between the sea and the terrace on which they stood they could just make out the line of the headlands.

"I think Credding's already got a theory," remarked Wendover suddenly. "He thinks that Severfield, by some means or other, was inveigled into this bungalow, struck down here, and having been dragged across this field, was thrown over the cliff. And — it is a very likely theory!"

"Yes," said Bridgwater. "But it argues the participation of more than one man in the crime! No one man, however strong and able, could have dragged Severneld's body three hundred yards! He was a heavy man — sixteen stone, I should say."

"Two men could do it," answered Wendover. "Well — a lonely spot! If Severfield really was knocked on the head in this house —"

Credding interrupted him by calling from the side they had originally approached; going back there they found him with an elderly man, who had also provided himself with a lantern.

"This is Mr. Fowler, gentlemen," said Credding. "Gardener by trade, and caretaker of this bit of property. Now if you'll let us in, and come in with us, Mr. Fowler," he continued jauntily, "we'll just see what there is to be seen. Been in lately yourself, Mr. Fowler?"

"Why, sir, no, I can't say as I have," replied Fowler, as he unlocked the door, and ushered the three men into a square hall. "No, sir — not this three or four weeks or so. My wife, she comes in once or twice a week, to look round — Monday morning she was in, sir."

"Monday morning, eh?" said Credding. "Just so! You didn't have anybody asking for the key on Monday evening, did you?"

"No, sir — ain't nobody asked for the key since last summer. This ain't what you might call a winter residence, sir."

"Still, it's to let," observed Credding. "Well, let's have a look at it."

There was little to be seen. A lounge-hall. Two sitting-rooms. Two bedrooms; a bathroom, a kitchen. All well and comfortably furnished — and all, as the detective was quick to remark, in apple-pie order. No sign of any struggle — nothing out of place — no sign whatever of recent occupancy — not even a trace of dirty boots.

"I suppose you didn't happen to see a light in here last Monday evening, Mr. Fowler?" inquired Credding suddenly.

"A light? In here, sir? No, indeed, I didn't, sir! Don't know how they could be, either! How could anybody get in with a light, sir?"

"I don't know," replied Credding. "But it's been reported to us that a light was seen in this place, moving about, at about nine o'clock — ten minutes past nine."

"Well, that's queer, sir!" said Fowler. "As I say, we've always had the key. It wasn't us, anyway. Nine o'clock, Monday night! — we was in bed, as we always are, that time o' night. Dear me! — I never heard of no light."

"Aye, well — you may hear yet," remarked Credding. "Evidently nothing's amiss — nothing's been touched. But who's the owner of this bungalow?"

"Belongs to Mrs. Rathbourne, sir — a widow lady. She built it two or three years ago. Lived in it a bit herself at first — then she left it."

"Do you know where Mrs. Rathbourne lives now?"

"Yes, sir. She lives at 570, Palmeira Avenue, Hove."

"Old lady?" suggested Credding.

"No, sir. What you call middlin' age, she is — maybe between fifty and sixty. Very nice lady is Mrs. Rathbourne."

"And I suppose this bungalow's let now and then?"

"It's never been let a great deal, sir. This last year, only once."

"Who was that to?"

"Well, sir, I couldn't tell you the name, for I never knew it! It was to a tallish, well-made gentleman and his lady — fine-looking woman she was. They had it for about a month — end of summer. But we saw next to nothing of them — they were in Brighton or somewhere all day. Seemed to use this bungalow only for sleeping."

"Then I suppose they took it from Mrs. Rathbourne herself?"

"Oh, yes, sir I Mrs. Rathbourne, she come along one day, and said she'd let the bungalow to a gentleman and his wife for a time — she didn't say how long — and they'd be coming to-morrow. That was all we knew about it — saw 'em now and then, to be sure. But that was always either early of a morning or laterish in an evening. Never rek'lect seein' of 'em in the day-time. I took the gentleman for a horse-racing party."

"Why, now?" asked Credding.

"Why, sir, he was one o' these here as dressed what they call loud — flash sort o' clothes, and white billycock hat, and, when they went out of a morning, he always had field-glasses slung over his shoulders. I've seen a many of his sort up there on the racecourse, time and again, sir."

"Well, whoever he was, he'd have a key, or keys, of this place," said Credding. "Did he give any keys up to you?"

"No, sir — he got the keys from Mrs. Rathbourne, and I suppose he gave 'em back to her. We'd no dealings with him, or his lady either. We never knew when they left, but they did leave, and as they didn't return we put up the card in the window again." Credding, after a few more words with the caretaker, led his companions back to the waiting cab, and bade the driver go to Palmeira Avenue. He was very silent during the drive from one side of Brighton to the other, but as they reached Hove he suddenly broke out in a sharp exclamation.

"I believe Severfield was murdered in that bungalow!" he said, bringing a hand down heavily on his knee. "I do! Or at any rate stunned by a blow. And, of course, there must have been two men at it. Or three! Well..."

The cab pulled up at 570, Palmeira Avenue just then, and Credding descended and rang the bell of a large house. The two men left in the cab watched him talking for some minutes to a smart parlourmaid; presently he came back.

"Mrs. Rathbourne is away," he said. "Wintering on the Riviera. At present she's at Bordighera — I've got her address — the Hotel Angleterre. I shall wire to her at once. Well — that's all for to-night. What can I do for you, gentlemen?"

"Drive us to the station, Credding," replied Wendover. "We'll get home to London."

"Knowing a great deal more, Mr. Wendover, than you did two hours ago!" said the detective as he gave the necessary order and got in.

"Gentlemen! — this is going to be as big a business as it's a bad one!"

"What will come next?" said the banker, half fretfully. "Most — trying!"

Credding made no reply. Nor did Wendover. But Wendover smiled quietly. Orridge, he thought, would come next.

Chapter IX
The Spanner

Late though it was when Credding set down the banker and the solicitor at the railway station, his own work was not done. Credding was one of those wise folk who believe that if a thing's got to be done, the time to do it is there and then. So he went off to the head post office, and after some thought as regards its wording, dispatched his telegram to Mrs. Rathbourne, asking her for particulars of her late tenant at Elvescot. And that done, and police head-quarters being close by, he turned in there, just, as he said, to see if there was anything that needed his attention before going home for the night.

"There's been a man here, asking for you," said the official to whom Credding presented himself. "Welford, who keeps that garage and repairing shop at the corner of the road turning down to Black Rock from the Newhaven and Rottingdean Road. Said he'd seen your name in the papers in connection with this Severfield affair, and believed he could tell you something of interest."

"Didn't he tell you?" asked Credding.

"No! — said you were the man he wanted. Because he wasn't sure that it was of any importance, and didn't want to make a fuss about it. Still — he thought it might be, and wouldn't mind telling you as a bit of private suggestion — just to see what you thought of it — see?"

Credding glanced at the clock. Not yet half-past ten. Welford might still be up.

"All right," he said. "I'll go there now."

He went out and chartered another cab and drove up to the corner of which he had been told. The garage was in darkness, but there was a light in a lower window of the adjacent house, and Credding, bidding his driver to wait, approached the door and knocked. A drawing back of bolts and undoing of locks prefaced the looking out of a man who, from the fact that he was without coat and vest and had taken off his boots, appeared to have been about to retire.

"Mr. Welford?" asked Credding. "Sorry to disturb you, but I hear you've been inquiring for me — Detective-Sergeant Credding."

"Come in, sir — come in!" said Welford. He led the way into a parlour, gave Credding a chair, and taking another himself smiled deprecatingly, as if not quite sure of the value of the information he had offered. "I don't know whether there's anything in it or not, Mr. Credding — I just called at the police-office on the chance, d'ye see?"

"I see," assented Credding. "And what is it?"

"Well, of course, I've read all this news in the papers about the affair of that Mr. Severfield," answered Welford. "I gather that the police — that you, yourself — think it's a case of murder?"

"I think so," said Credding.

"Not accident?" suggested the garage proprietor.

"I've said — murder!" replied Credding, firmly. "Just — murder! Good grounds, too, for that belief!"

"Well, if it was murder, somebody murdered him," remarked Welford. "And so what I can tell you might have something to do with it. It's just this. The night before Hopperson — I know Hopperson well enough, but I haven't mentioned this to him: fact is, until now, I've mentioned it to no one — before Hopperson found that man lying dead on the beach — Monday night it was, of course — there was a man came to my garage door and asked me if I'd a spanner I could sell him. He pointed to his car drawn up on the side of the road, going towards Rottingdean, perhaps twenty or thirty yards away: he wanted the spanner for that. I found him an old one and charged him something — not much — I forget what. He went off with it to the car. I saw there was another man in the car with him: he got out when the first man went back, and they were both tinkering at the car for some little time. I was thinking of going up the road, to see if I could be of any use, when they both got in again and drove off. And, of course, that was the last I saw of them. Now, you'll not think much of that bit of an incident, Mr. Credding, no doubt! — but there's more to it. When this man came up to the door and asked for a spanner, I had an idea that I knew him — by sight. But I couldn't place him — nohow! Still, I was sure his face and all about him was familiar — yet, I couldn't think where and when I'd seen him. And it wasn't till to-day that it suddenly flashed across me — I did know him! He was a man who, for a short time at the end of last summer, had a bungalow up the road here — Elvescot."

Credding, who was listening intently, gave no sign of suddenly aroused interest. He merely nodded.

"I never knew that man's name, or anything about him," continued Welford. "But I saw him now and again. He hadn't a car when he was here at that bungalow. Leastways, I never saw him in one. But at that time I've seen him and the lady he was with in the bus, or on foot. Queer that I didn't recognise him when he turned up the other night, but, you see, I'd fogotten all about him. However, I'm sure he was the man who was at Elvescot.

"You can describe him, of course?" suggested Credding.

"Oh, yes! A big, fleshy man, broad face, very dark, shortish moustache. Sporty sort — when he was at Elvescot I took him for a bookmaker. That sort, you know — rather loud and flashy. Of course, the other night he was a good deal muffled up, for driving — it was a coldish night."

"What time was it when he called?" inquired the detective.

"Half-past-eight — exactly."

"And how long was he there with his car — on the roadside?"

"Maybe ten minutes longer."

"And he went off towards —"

"Rottingdean. The car was headed that way when he came after the spanner. He'd evidently come from Brighton."

"You didn't see the other man's face?"

"No — not at all. Too far off — all I saw was that there was a second man with the first. A tall man, as far as I could see, but not so broadly built. This man I'm talking of is a big man."

"I suppose the car was too far off for you to take any particular notice of it?" suggested Credding. "You wouldn't be able to identify it?"

"No, I couldn't identify it. But it was a biggish car — a four-seater. And light coloured — grey, I fancy."

Credding considered this information awhile in silence.

"Is there anywhere along the road here where a man could leave a car for a while, unobserved?" he asked at last. "Any bylane, for instance?"

"Oh, yes!" replied Welford. "There's a lane turning up toward the downs, a little beyond Elvescot, on the opposite side of the road, of course, into which you could turn a car and leave it, quite safely, especially at night."

Credding sat, silently thinking, a little longer. At last he rose.

"Well, I'm obliged to you," he said. "I'll go into this. Meanwhile, Mr. Welford, just keep it to yourself. There may be something in it: there may not. Anyhow, I'm glad to have heard what you have to say. And maybe I'll be up this way again tomorrow."

Credding felt more certain than he let Welford see that there was something in this story, and he would have gone straight on with his investigation of it there and then if midnight had not been approaching. As it was he was back at Black Rock by nine o'clock next morning, alone — looking for the lane which the garage proprietor had spoken of. He found that easily enough; a narrow lane running between high banks upwards toward the downs; its mouth about two hundred yards east of the bungalow. It was not the sort of lane into which anyone would take a motorcar at any time in the usual course of events, for as it went further inland it developed into deep ruts and mud, and was evidently nothing but an accommodation road to certain fields. But near the entrance to it, where the surface was firmer, Credding had no difficulty in tracing the recent marks of a certain make of tire — there they were, plain enough; there, too, were still more evident marks, where the car had rested in soft earth. There was no doubt about it — somebody, quite recently, had driven a heavyish car into that lane for about twenty yards, and had left it there some little time. The traces of the driving-in, and of the backing-out, were unmistakable.

From inspecting these obvious marks, Credding went back to the bungalow, and passing through its garden, walked slowly across the headland towards the place beneath which Hopperson had found Severfield's dead body. And there, walking about, his old telescope under his arm, he came across Hopperson himself.

Hopperson, always a chatty man, greeted the detective in friendly fashion: they had not met since the morning of the inquest.

"Having another look round, Mr. Credding?" he asked.

"Anything new yet?"

"Not much," replied Credding. Then feeling that Hopperson was a thoroughly dependable man, to whom it was quite safe to talk freely, he added. "Still — there's a bit." He turned, pointing to the bungalow above them. "You know that place above there, I reckon, Hopperson?"

"Elvescot? Yes, I know it, Mr. Credding," replied the ex-Navy man. "What of it?"

"Do you remember a gentleman and lady living in it for a bit last summer?"

"Yes! They weren't there so long — maybe, a month."

"Did you ever hear the name?"

"No — never, to my recollection. I believe they did little more than use it for sleeping in. Weren't seen about much, anyway."

"Still, you remember what they were like?"

"Oh, yes, Mr. Credding. She was a good-looking, fair-complexioned woman, lightish hair — what they call buxom. He was a big, stoutish man, full face, dark moustache. Oh, I remember 'em, well enough."

"I'll tell you something," said Credding. And as they strolled about, above the gap at which Severfield had fallen, or through which he had been flung, he began to tell Hopperson the Welford story. But he had not got far when Hopperson stopped him with a sharp exclamation.

"Spanner!" he cried. "Why, Mr. Credding, I — I found a spanner!"

Credding pulled himself up and turned quickly on his companion.

"You found a spanner?" he exclaimed "Where — when?"

"When — I found him!" replied Hopperson. "At least, not so many minutes afterwards. You see, after I'd found him, a neighbour of mine came along, and I sent him off to telephone to your people. When he'd gone I walked round about the body — down there," he continued, pointing to the beach beneath them. "It was a bitterly cold morning, as you may remember — I walked about to keep myself warm. And in walking about, I found a spanner lying on the shingle, some yards from the dead man. I picked it up and put it in my pocket — I've often found similar articles on this shore — all sorts o' things get washed up. This looked as if it had been washed up — it was old, and it was rusty."

"Good heavens, why didn't you tell me at once!" exclaimed Credding. "If I'd known" — he paused, reflecting that even if he had known, he could then have done nothing. "Well?" he went on. "Where is it?"

"At my house, in a box full of old stuff," answered Hopperson. "I flung it in there when I went home, and I've never seen it since. You think —"

"Never mind what I think!" said Credding. "Come on! — where is your house? — let me have that spanner."

Hopperson led the way to his cottage and into a shed at the back where he kept all sorts of miscellaneous odds and ends. He threw back the lid of an old box.

"There you are!" he said. "That's it! Just where I threw it, when I came in that morning. Of course, if I'd only known —"

"Oh, well, better late than never!" remarked Credding. "I've got it now. And I reckon that it was this that Severfield was knocked down with! Stunned! — before being thrown over the cliff. All right — now we'll step along to Welford's, and see if he recognises it as the one he sold."

Welford recognised the spanner readily enough. It was an old one, he said, that had been knocking about his shop, little used, for some time — he'd chanced to see it when the big man asked for one and had offered it at once — it would do for what he wanted, said the big man. It was rusted, then, he added, but not so much so as now.

Leaving Hopperson to go home, with an admonition to silence, Credding got the garage proprietor to accompany him up the road to the narrow lane in which he had found the marks of wheels.

"Look at those, now!" he said. "I supposeyou can tell what make of tyre it is that caused those marks?"

"Oh, yes, Mr. Credding!" replied Welford, readily. "Michelin! And it's very easy to see that no car's ever been in this lane before! That's certain."

"It was run in for a purpose!" muttered Credding, with a grim smile. "Well — just keep things to yourself a bit."

He went back to the police head-quarters — to put the spanner away in safety, and to find a wire from Wendover asking him to go up to town at once. Without a moment's delay he set out for the station, philosophically reflecting on that excellent dispensation of Providence which has separated Brighton from London by only one hour's railway run.

Chapter X
The Residuary Legatee

Credding, shown into Wendover's private room as soon as he arrived at his office, found the solicitor alone.

"Good of you to come at once," said Wendover, motioning him to a chair by his desk. "We seem scarcely to have parted! — still, I've got some information for you which I thought you'd better hear immediately. It's not pressing, though — if you've any since we left you last night?"

"A bit," replied Credding. "Perhaps I'd better tell mine first." He gave the solicitor a rapid account of his discoveries at Black Rock. "What do you make of that, now?" he concluded. "Seems to me we've a distinct clue!"

"The thing is to find out who the man is who lived at Elvescot for a time," said Wendover. "You haven't heard from the owner — what's her name?"

"Mrs. Rathbourne. No — but I expect to hear during the day," answered Credding. "I suppose she'll know — she ought to know. It's not likely she'd let her house without knowing something of the man she let it to — she'd probably have some reference. I shall find him!"

"The bother about all this," remarked Wendover, "is that we know so very little of Severfield and his doings since he came to London. They know very little indeed at the bank. Colinrake is the only person who seems to have known much of him — and for various reasons we can't ask Colinrake searching questions — at present, anyway. For anything we know Severfield may have known a good many people here — and some of them may have been doubtful characters. It's certainly a very suspicious circumstance that this man who rented Mrs. Rathbourne's bungalow should have been back in its neighbourhood on the very evening, and at the very hour, that Severfield was undoubtedly somewhere about there. It looks as if a meeting had been arranged between them. You'll have to get hold of that man, Credding!"

"I shall find him!" repeated Credding. "I'm only waiting for Mrs. Rathbourne's answer to my telegram to get to work on that matter. But — your news?"

Wendover smiled as he touched a bell on his desk.

"To tell you the truth, I scarcely know what it is myself yet!" he replied. "I set my clerk, Orridge, to find out whatever he could about the young lady to whom Severfield left all his money; when I came in this morning, he told me that he'd certain facts to report, and they were by no means creditable to the young lady. So I told him I'd send for you, and he could defer giving his exact story until you turned up."

"He's to be depended upon, I suppose, this clerk of yours?" asked Credding.

"You can take my word for that!" answered Wendover with a confident laugh. "Orridge, in my opinion, ought to have been in your profession! He's a human ferret! — he can get hold of information where most men would fail. And he has a peculiar knowledge of people connected with my profession — young as he looks, he'd been in two or three solicitors' offices before he came to me — and as he's an inveterate gossip, or rather a keen-witted listener to other people's gossip, there's precious little that he doesn't know. Oh, yes, you can depend on whatever Orridge has to tell us!"

The clerk came in just then, and Credding, after a good look at him, decided that Wendover was about right in his reckoning. He settled himself to listen with interest.

"Go ahead, Orridge," said Wendover. "All about this Miss Beatrix Greville, of course! You've made some discoveries?"

"A few, sir," replied Orridge. "Not so very difficult to get hold of, either. To begin with, that isn't the young lady's real name. Leastways, it isn't the name she was born with, though, to be sure, she's called herself Beatrix Greville for so many years that I suppose she's acquired a title to it. But she was born Beatrix Grevelli. Her father was a musician — an Italian. He played the 'cello in the orchestra of the Hyperion Theatre for a good many years, and he married a woman who was employed as a dresser there, a Miss Jane Brown."

"Didn't Miss Greville say in her evidence at the inquest that she now had an aunt. Miss Henrietta Brown, living with her?" asked Wendover.

"She did — and she has," replied Orridge. "Elderly old party, quite respectable and, I should say, from what I've learnt, quite under her niece's thumb; bit of camouflage, having the old lady there, I think."

"I see!" said Wendover. "Well — and the father's dead, eh?"

"Father's dead, and mother," replied Orridge. "Both died when this girl was about fifteen or sixteen — seven years ago. As regards herself, she's been connected with the theatre from childhood — dancing. She was in pantomimes, regularly, as one of a children's troupe. Later on she was in the ballet — don't know if she ever got into the front row! But she was a ballet-dancer for years — called herself Beatrix Greville all that time. And she was known to associate with Colinrake."

"What do you mean by that?" asked Creddling. "How did she assosiate with Colinfrake?"

"Colinrake," answered Orridge, "appears, from all I've gathered up, to have been fond of the society of young ladies of that profession — girls employed in the ballet, or as supernumeraries, choristers, and so on. Sort of chap who took such girls out to supper, and that sort of thing. I mean that he and Miss Greville were seen in each other's company a good deal. Bit of a man about town is Colinrake — club man — that is, sporting clubs. Bohemian — if that's the right word."

"Well, about this young lady?" said Wendover. "Go on — if there's more."

"Lots more!" responded the clerk dryly. "About two years or so ago. Miss Greville seems to have cut the stage, and to have gone to Colinrake's office as his secretary. That's what she told us at the inquest. She said there, too, that she'd learned shorthand and typing. If she ever did, I haven't been able to find out that she did, or where it was! But I've had a confidential talk with a friend of mine who was at Colinrake's for a few months last year. He says that Miss Greville was merely ornamental. She professed to be Colinrake's private secretary, and she had a small office opening out of his, and she perhaps did a bit. But he says she knew no shorthand at all, and she couldn't type a letter, though she was a good hand at getting afternoon tea ready. She and Colinrake always went out to lunch together, and generally came to the office together of a morning, and left together in the evening. It was a bit of a joke with the other clerks — two of 'em — that she was there at all, for there wasn't work for the lot; that was why this chap I'm talking of didn't stay very long."

"Find out anything as regards her relations with Colinrake after Severfield came on the scene?" inquired Wendover.

"This much. It's quite true that not so very long after Severfield came to London — according to the dates we've had given — Miss Greville and her aunt took possession of the flat they're in now. But she seems, as far as I can make out — I'm only on the edge of things yet, you know — to have continued going regularly to Colinrake's office, and she and Colinrake have been seen about together as much as usual — lunching together, and so on. The engagement to Mr. Severfield, if there was one," concluded Orridge with a sly smile, "seems to have made precious little difference!"

"That all?" inquired Credding.

"All about what you might call the first stage," replied Orridge. "Up to Mr. Severfield's death. But there's more. Last night I thought I'd watch outside Miss Greville's flats, just to see if I could spot anything. I spotted a good deal!"

"Go on with it," said Wendover. "I thought you were probably saving the best of it!"

"It may be the most important," replied Orridge quietly. "There are certainly some strange features about it. I took up a convenient position outside these flats in which Miss Greville lives, just about dusk. I've been pretty well used to watching — Mr. Credding there'll know what I mean — in my time. Well, nothing happened until about a quarter to eight. Then Colinrake and Miss Greville came up in a taxicab. They went in, and I'd a good view of 'em. She was dressed as she was at the inquest at Brighton — mourning clothes, you know. I waited about until nine o'clock. Then Colinrake came out — alone. He walked away in a fashion that suggested that he wasn't coming back. However, being a chap with, I believe, an unlimited stock of patience, I thought I'd wait a while longer. And I had my reward! I'd got where I could see into the hall of those flats, and at about ten o'clock I suddenly saw Miss Greville appear in it, talking to the hall-porter. She evidently told him to get her a taxi — he came outside to whistle for one; she followed him to the steps, and I'd a full view of her."

Orridge paused, smiling at his recollection.

"She wasn't in mourning garments then, gentlemen — not she!" he continued. "I saw at once that she was going to a ball, or some 'do', of that sort — dressed up to the mark, she was, with a fancy cloak over her. The cab came up, and in she popped. I made after her, cautiously, to the corner; there were more cabs there, and I jumped into the first, gave the driver the order to follow her cab, and off we went. And, to cut it short, I ran her down!"

"To where?" asked Credding.

"Amaryllis Club," replied Orridge. "That's where!"

"I'm not as intimately acquainted with London as I am with Brighton, young man," remarked the detective. "Mr. Wendover here may know where and what the Amaryllis Club is —"

"Not I!" said Wendover. "Never heard of it!"

"It's just what you please to call it," answered Orridge. "Night club — dancing club — social club — in Hallam Street. I knew of it. It's a good reputation — never been any rows, raids, or anything of that sort in connection with it. Well conducted, you understand. I've heard, for instance, that you can't get a drink there except at the proper times — strict management. I fancy it really is a dancing club — where people go who really want to dance — anyway, it's never been pulled up."

"Well — and she went there, eh?" asked Credding.

"She went there — I watched her go in. I saw a good many others go in, too. Men and women — chiefly young. And having seen her go in, I knew she'd be safe for a while, so I went and got some supper and rested a bit. I know these places and their doings, and the habits of those who go there; I knew that two o'clock in the morning would be a likely time to see more. Of course, I was back before that, and before two o'clock came I'd fixed things with a taxi-man, so that if I did spot my lady again I could follow her once more; might as well make a job of it while I was at it!"

"Good man!" said Credding approvingly. "Well?"

"Well, just as I'd expected, she came out about a quarter past two. Not alone. She'd a tall young fellow, in evening dress, with her — seemed very pally with each other, too. They walked a bit down the street, and then got a cab — I got mine, and we followed, discreetly. She and this chap she was with drove to the corner of her flats. She got out and went in — he didn't. He drove off — west. And I paid my man and went home. That's the lot — so far!"

Credding rubbed his hands together and looked at Wendover.

"Nice goings-on, Mr. Wendover, on the part of a young lady whose fiance has just been murdered and whose body's still awaiting burial!" he said. "I think there's a lot that's got to be inquired into about this Miss Greville and her interest in that will! And by the by," he continued, "if there's any uneasiness or suspicion about things, how will matters stand about that will? I gather that Mr. Bridgwater doesn't like the look of the affair?"

"He doesn't!" said Wendover. "But the trouble is that we don't know of any relation of Severfield's. If that will's all right, and this young woman, as sole executor, proves the will, the bankers can't refuse to hand over the money in their hands when probate is produced to them. Only a person having an interest or asserting an interest can interfere; we don't know of any such person. Of course, if the bankers get serious cause for suspicion, we could communicate with the Attorney-General, as representing the Crown, and if he thought necessary he could oppose the grant of probate. But there's another way — if evidence arrives at the inquest which strengthens the suspicion that there's been foul play, not only about Severfield's death, but as regards the execution of the will, the police can take some action in the matter. But — has there? Colinrake, of course, asserts that the will is absolutely in order. Now if Severfield really was murdered by some person of whose identity you, for instance, know nothing positive so far, that won't affect the will — if properly executed."

"You may be quite sure it'll be properly executed, Mr. Wendover, if Colinrake had it in hand!" said Orridge. "Trust him! But may I put in a word? Well, then, don't be squeamish about facing ugly facts. Here's a very rich man makes a will leaving all he has to a young woman, and he's scarcely made it before he's cleverly put out of the way! Eh? I think Mr. Credding sees my point."

Credding made no answer. He sat staring at the fire a while.

"I'll tell you what it is, Mr. Wendover," he said suddenly. "I think I shall transfer my sphere of action here a bit. Now, I've a fancy to see the inside of this dancing club — Orridge here no doubt knows how one can get in?"

"Easy as winking!" said Orridge. "I know!"

"Then I suggest," continued Credding" that — say on the third night from this — we 'all three go there — evening dress, I suppose? Let's call that a fixture. Severfield will have been buried by then, and the young lady will no doubt want a little relaxation — anyhow, I want to see her at that club"

Chapter XI
The Green Bag

The detective rose, buttoned his coat, and, picking up his umbrella, gave signs of departure. But Wendover motioned him to his seat again.

"Wait a minute, Credding," he said. "I don't suppose you're in any great hurry. And it's just occurred to me — since you are here, and since Orridge already knows a great deal of this case — do you mind telling him a bit more? Orridge is as secret as the grave —"

Credding sat down again.

"Such as — what?" he asked.

"Tell him what you told Mr. Bridgwater and myself yesterday, when we came down to you," replied Wendover. "I mean the working-man story, and the bus-conductor's, and so on, and what you've told me this morning. You see," he went on, "if we're all going to investigate this affair, there are two people we particularly want to get hold of: one, the mysterious woman who was with Severfield that Monday evening; the other, the man who lived in the bungalow, Elvescot, for a time, and seems to have been back in its neighbourhood at about the time Severfield was murdered. I'd like be put in possession of all that's known up to now — eh?"

"Oh, I've no objection — it's between ourselves," answered Credding. "And I'm always only too glad to get a hint or a suggestion. Well, the facts Mr. Wendover refers to are these," he went on, turning to Orridge. "You listen carefully to 'em —"

He went on to give a concise account of the statements made — first by Simpson, the taxicab driver; second by Wright, the general labourer; third by Brownson, the bus-conductor. But he had scarcely finished retailing Brownson's story when a sudden gleam of recognition shot over Orridge's sharp features, and an equally sudden exclamation came from his thin lips.

"Bright green bag, with queer gold figures on it!" exclaimed Orridge. "Why, that's Mrs. Emerson! Dead sure! Leastways, I mean, that's her bag!"

A dead silence fell on the three. Wendover looked at Credding; Credding looked at Wendover. But Credding's glance quickly shifted itself to the clerk.

"And who may be Mrs. Emerson?" he asked quietly. "Somebody known to you?"

"She's the proprietor of that place we've been talking about," replied Orridge. "The Amaryllis Club. Registered proprietor. I know her — by sight. And the green bag, too. Saw her there with it last night. Oh, yes — Mrs. Emerson. Anyhow, she has a green bag like that — I noticed it particularly."

Credding looked again at Wendover, and smiled cynically.

"There you are, you see!" he exclaimed. "Now if you hadn't suggested I should post Orridge up, we shouldn't have heard that! — yet, at any rate. Coincidence! — Lord bless you, I'm always coming across coincidence! — the world's full of coincidence! Well — well! Of course, there may be more than one bright green bag —"

"It's a highly uncommon one, that I'm talking about," said Orridge. "And there's another thing — this Mrs. Emerson fits in exactly with the descriptions you've had from both Simpson and Brownson — particularly from Brownson. Lay anything she's the woman! She was in furs last night — I saw her in and out of the Amaryllis two or three times. Besides, I've seen her before — I knew her as proprietor. Making a fortune out of that club, they say."

"I must have a look at her," said Credding. "If we could get her private address —"

Orridge jumped to his feet and turned to a table on which were ranged a number of up-to-date reference books.

"Easy enough, that," he murmured, seizing on a thick volume and turning over its pages. "As she's the registered proprietor of the Amaryllis Club, her private address is bound to be given. Here you are — she lives at 571, Queensborough Terrace, Bayswater. And she's described as a widow."

"I must have a look at her," repeated Credding. He stood staring out of the window for a minute or two, as if in deep thought. "I was just wondering," he said, suddenly turning on Wendover, "if it mightn't be well to wire or telephone to our people at Brighton, telling them to get hold of Brownson and send him up here — to see if he could identify her as the lady he saw in his bus. And — perhaps Simpson, too."

"You needn't bother yourself, Mr. Credding," said Orridge. "If you and Mr. Wendover'll leave it to me, I'll engage to bring Mrs. Emerson here, to this office, at five o'clock this afternoon. How will that suit you?"

Wendover laughed as he saw the look of astonishment on the detective's face.

"He'll do it, Credding, if he says he will," he remarked. "Trust him!"

"I'd like to know how he'll do it!" exclaimed Credding. He gave Orridge another keen inspection. "Seems to me you've a pretty good opinion of your own powers, my lad!" he said. "Now how will you get Mrs. Emerson here?"

"Give her her choice of coming quietly with me for a little private talk here with Mr. Wendover, or having a visit from the police — from you! — at the club this evening," replied Orridge promptly. "She'll come!"

"Supposing she isn't the woman who was at Brighton on the evening in question?" suggested Credding. "What then?"

"I shall make sure of that before I give her her choice of alternatives," answered Orridge. "You leave that to me!"

"Yes, leave it to him, Credding," said Wendover. "All right, Orridge," he continued, nodding to the clerk, "Off you go! Five o'clock — here. He'll bring her!" he went on, presently, when Orridge had gone away without wasting more words. "And it will be a wise move — I've something in view, and if you'll sit down again, I'll tell you what it is." He proceeded to recapitulate the story which Marsland had told him and Bridgwater. "Now, Credding!" he concluded. "Suppose this Mrs. Emerson is one of those two women — either the wife or the sister? Eh? And why not? She was somebody — I mean the woman at Brighton was somebody — that Severfield knew. Anyway" — here he looked at his watch — "there's nice time to do it, and I'm going to wire to Marsland to come along here this afternoon and have a look at this Mrs. Emerson — if he recognises her as one of the two sisters he spoke of, I think we shall have done a fine day's work."

"You seem to be pretty certain that he will!" said Credding.

"I shouldn't wonder! But I've some reason. The woman who was with Severfield during the ride in the taxicab from Brighton to the end of Ovingdean Lane must have seen no end in the newspapers about the affair. Why has she not come forward? Because she has a reason for keeping herself in the background — because she doesn't want her name to appear. Why? Surely because of some secret! Well, there must have been a secret about the sudden running away from Severfield's sheep-station of the two sisters told about by Marsland. Is that secret and this secret all one? Possibly — perhaps probably. Anyway, I'm confident that Orridge will bring Mrs. Emerson here at five o'clock this afternoon, and I think we shall find that she's the woman spoken of by Simpson and by Brownson, for the green bag seems pretty conclusive, and I'm going to get Marsland here, and Bridgwater, too — you go and amuse yourself for an hour or two and be back here in good time. Then... we'll see!"

Credding went away and amused himself by taking two hours over his dinner instead of one. Even then he had plenty of time to kill; he got rid of some of it by telephoning to Brighton, to inquire if any answer had yet arrived from Mrs. Rathbourne at Bordighera. But none had come, nor had he been rung up from Brighton when he returned to Wendover's office at a quarter to five.

Bridgwater was with Wendover when Credding entered the solicitor's room, but there was no sign of the man from Bedford.

"I've had no reply from Marsland," said Wendover, seeing Credding look round. "He may be away. Still, if Orridge succeeds in capturing the lady, I think the results will be profitable."

"You take a rose-coloured view of it!" said Credding, a little cynically. "But I suppose you know Orridge's powers of persuasion — or coercion! — better than I do."

He walked over to the window and looked out on the street. "By George!" he exclaimed suddenly. "He's got her! They're here! — he's handing her out of a cab! Clever chap, that, Mr. Wendover! — to tell you the truth, I scarcely expected he'd do it!"

"I did!" said Wendover. "Now then-caution! No alarming her. This is an absolutely private and confidential affair, you know —"

The door opened, and Orridge, suave and bland, ushered in an elegantly-dressed handsome woman who carried a bright green bag in her gloved hand, and looked round the room with a well-bred but very evident inquisitive-ness which rapidly took in one man after the other of the three who rose and bowed to her.

"Mrs. Emerson, sir," said Orridge, in his best manner.

"How do you do, Mrs. Emerson," said Wendover, drawing forward an easy chair. "I am very much obliged to you for coming to see me. My clerk has no doubt explained —"

"In such a fashion — though quite kindly, I'm sure — that he left me no choice!" interrupted Mrs. Emerson, taking her seat. "I'm a pretty well-experienced woman of the world, Mr. Wendover, and I soon saw that if I didn't come here, I should have to expect — somebody arriving to see me! So — here I am! And — these gentlemen?"

"Mr. Bridgwater — the late Mr. Severfield's banker," said Wendover." Detective-Sergeant Credding, of Brighton."

"Police, eh?" said Mrs. Emerson "Well — "

"Detective-Sergeant Credding is not here — exactly — in any professional capacity, Mrs. Emerson," said Wendover. "Make your mind at ease — this is a perfectly informal meeting, and anything said here is to be said in strict confidence and privacy. Let us go straight to the root of the matter. We believe that you are the lady who got into a taxicab at the bottom of East Street, in Brighton, in company with Mr. Severfield on the Monday evening on which he met his death and rode with him as far as the end of Ovingdean Lane, where the man who drove the cab says he left his two passengers talking by the roadside. Now, will you be kind enough to tell us — are you that lady?"

Mrs. Emerson looked round the semicircle of men intently watching her.

"Yes!" she answered promptly. "I am!" Wendover sighed with evident relief.

"Thank you!" he said. "That simplifies matters. It'll simplify matters still more — as far as I'm concerned — if you answer another direct question with the same readiness. Do you know anything whatever of the causes of Mr. Severfield's death?"

"Nothing! Nothing whatever! When I left Mr. Severfield that night, he was, as far as I could see, in perfect health. I was amazed when I heard of his death. But, of course, I thought he had met with an accident."

"You knew Mr. Severfield, of course?"

"I had not seen Mr. Severfield for quite twenty years, Mr. Wendover. I met him by pure chance in Brighton. We had not met five minutes when we entered that taxicab."

"And may I ask — where had you seen him last, before that, Mrs. Emerson — twenty years ago?"

Before Mrs. Emerson could answer, a clerk entered the room and approaching Wendover, whispered to him: Wendover made a whispered reply. The clerk went back to the door, and held it open, and Credding, following his movements, saw an elderly man enter.

"Come in — Mr. Marsland!" said Wendover, purposely pronouncing the name in clear tones. "Orridge! — a chair for Mr. Marsland."

At the first mention of the visitor's name, Credding saw Mrs. Emerson start; at the second she turned sharply in the direction of the door. And Marsland, advancing, and coming face to face with her, started, too.

"Good heavens!" he exclaimed. "Miss May! I — I can't be mistaken?"

Mrs. Emerson turned quickly on Wendover.

"This looks very much like some trap you are laying —" she began. "You assured me —"

"There is no trap, Mrs. Emerson," interrupted Wendover. "It is just that recent events are bringing things together. This gentleman, Mr. Marsland, on hearing of Mr. Severfield's death, came forward to give Mr. Bridgwater and myself some information about Severfield's marriage at the time he, Mr. Marsland, was his neighbour in New South Wales. Mr. Marsland told us all he knew about the young Mrs. Severfield and her sister. Miss May. And — he evidently recognises you as Miss May. Am I right in believing that Mr. Severfield himself did — when you met in Brighton the other night?"

Mrs. Emerson had remained looking at Marsland. She turned at last, slowly, and gave her attention to Wendover.

"Am I still to believe that you pledge yourself that this is all confidential?" she asked.

"You are. It is," asserted Wendover. "Strictly."

"Yes, then. Severfield did recognise me — as his sister-in-law. Of course, I soon told him that I had been married, and was now a widow. I may as well tell you all about it. We hadn't met for twenty years — as I said. It was pure chance that we met. I had gone down to Brighton to see a friend of mine who is very ill — at Rottingdean — in a house at the west end of Rottingdean. Severfield told me he, too, was going that way, he had an appointment to meet a man."

Chapter XII
Mrs. Emerson Talks

Mrs. Emerson paused for a moment, and before she could go on, Wendover signed to her to wait. '

"A moment, Mrs. Emerson! You say Severfield told you, almost as soon as you met him, that he had an appointment with a man. Now please think — did he mention the man's name?"

"No! He mentioned no name."

"Did he say where the appointment was to be kept?"

"No! He merely said he'd an appointment in the direction in which I was going, and offered me a lift."

"And you rode together as far as the end of Ovingdean Lane? Why did the cab stop there?"

"At my wish. The house I was going to visit is only some fifty or sixty yards past that, as you go towards Rottingdean. I asked to have the cab pulled up there. We both got out, and remained talking for a few minutes by the side of the road. Then we parted. I went on to my friend's house, and Severfield turned back, walking in the direction of Brighton. That was the last I saw of him."

"Did he ever, while you were with him, give you any indication — any at all — of where he was going, or who it was he was going to meet?"

"Not the slightest! Never mentioned it! We were talking the whole time of — well, of affairs in the past."

Wendover glanced at the banker.

"The past," he said, turning to Mrs. Emerson, "may, in this case, have a good deal to do with the present. Have you any objection to talking about the past — as far as it relates to Severfield, Mrs. Emerson?"

"It depends on what you want me to talk about," Mrs. Emerson replied. "I have no objection whatever to talking about my past. That's all clean and clear — and above board. What do you want to know?"

"Just this, if you please," answered Wendover, "and purely because of its relationship to Severfield. Why did you and your sister run away from him? — as, according to Mr. Marsland —"

"According to what was told to me," interrupted Marsland.

"According to what Mr. Marsland heard — you did," said Wendover. "Will you tell us something about that?"

"What has that got to do with this?" demanded Mrs. Emerson sharply. "I don't see —"

"It may have a good deal to do with it," replied Wendover. "Anyway," he added, seeing that she still hesitated, "it's a matter that will have to be inquired into. The late Mr. Severfield, Mrs. Emerson, was a man of great wealth. Your sister, we learn, was married to him."

Mrs. Emerson considered things for a moment.

"I don't mind going back to all that if this really is a private conversation," she said at last. "I don't know how much Mr. Marsland has told you? My sister certainly was married to Mr. Severfield. I'd better tell you all about it, I suppose, though it's raking up the past in a way that's highly unpleasant to me. You see — if I'm to begin at the beginning — my sister and I, as mere girls, were pretty well known on the music-hall stage. Our real name was that by which Mr. Marsland called me just now — May. Our stage name was Maybury — but we were usually known — announced on the bills and programmes, you know — as Rebbie and Rhona. My sister's Christian name is Rhona; mine Rebecca. We came of a family connected with the stage, and we were both well qualified to look after our own business affairs. When I was twenty, and Rhona a year younger, we went to South Africa: we appeared there in Cape Town, and at Johannesburg. Then we went to Australia, and after a few weeks in Melbourne we went on to Sydney. And there we met Severfield. Severfield fell in love with Rhona — he gave us no peace. He told us he was a very rich man, said he only meant to stay awhile at his place up-country, and that he was going to buy a steam-yacht and go all over the world, and he pressed us to go with him — both of us, Rhona, of course, to be Mrs. Severfield. I think she was carried away by his impetuousness; he was a forceful man. Anyway, she married him — quite suddenly — and we went off with him to his sheep-station. That's where Mr. Marsland, of course, saw us — but Mr. Marsland will remember that he only saw a little."

"What I saw was — occasional," said Marsand.

"So that Mr. Marsland didn't know the real truth," continued Mrs. Emerson. "And that was that the marriage was an absolute failure — the biggest mistake two people could have made! There wasn't a taste in common between Severfield and my sister — and, when you came to live with him, he was by no means either pleasant or easy to get on with — far from it. And in the end — which wasn't long in coming — we took advantage of Severfield's temporary absence from home, and ran away. We made straight for Sydney, caught a boat just leaving for San Francisco, and came back to England by way of the United States. From the time we left the sheep-station I never saw Severfield — nor heard of him — until we met, accidentally, at Brighton."

"Do you know if your sister has ever seen him?" asked Wendover.

"I can say positively that she never has," declared Mrs. Emerson. "Nor heard of him, either. That is absolute!"

"Where is your sister?"

"That I shall not say. I shall not tell you anything whatever about my sister — without her consent. I have no objection to telling anything about myself: I've nothing to conceal! A year or two after we came back to England, I married Mr. Emerson — he was connected, in management, with my own profession — and he died three years ago."

"I gather that your sister is alive?" suggested Wendover.

"My sister is alive."

"Did you tell Severfield that?"

"I told Severfield, as we rode together in the cab that night, just about what I have told you. I told him she was alive, but that I wouldn't say one word about her, nor tell him where she was, without her consent. And what I said to him I repeat to you! I shall tell nothing about her — until I have had an opportunity of seeing her and ascertaining her wishes."

"Did Severfield tell you anything of his private affairs, Mrs. Emerson?"

"No — except that he was in London."

"Did he tell you that he was thinking of marrying?"

"No! How could he, when I told him his wife was alive?"

"He probably thought she was dead. But, still, he didn't give you any idea that he'd been thinking of marrying somebody else?"

"Certainly not! never mentioned such a thing!"

"Did he tell you he was going to settle in England?"

"On the contrary, he said he was very soon going away again — to South America."

"Well, about that ride in the cab, Mrs. Emerson? You told us just now that the cab was pulled up at the end of Ovingdean Lane at your request?"

"Yes; the house I was going to visit is not far from that — a new, or newish house, between Ovingdean Lane and the beginning of Rottingdean. It is called "Channelcroft.' It belongs to a friend of mine — Mrs. Braithwaite. She is ill. That's why I went there — to see her. I'd gone down from London on purpose, and had just had dinner at a restaurant in East Street, before going on there, when I met Severfield."

"You and Severfield remained talking, at the roadside, after the cab left you, I think. How long?"

"Two or three minutes. I arranged to lunch with him at the Savoy Hotel, two days later. Then we parted — as I've already said, he turned back towards Brighton, walking, of course — I went on to 'Channelcroft.' I remained at 'Channelcroft' forty minutes, then I left to catch the bus at the hotel at Rottingdean. That was the 9.30 bus. I went back to Brighton by it, and caught the 10.20 express to Victoria."

"You're quite sure that Severfield never gave you any idea as to where he was going, nor as to the man he was to meet?"

"Certain! Beyond saying that he was going that way — Rottingdean way — to meet a man, he said nothing."

"Well, Mrs. Emerson, the real object of all this, as you've probably guessed before now, is to find out, if possible, where Severfield was going when he met you, and who it was that he was to meet there. You evidently can't help us on that most important point. But you can give us some information on another, I think. Now, you are the registered proprietor of the Amaryllis Club, aren't you?"

"I am! The best conducted place of its sort in London!"

"So I'm given to understand, and I congratulate you on its excellent character. Well, no doubt you're familiar with the people who go there?"

"With those who are there regularly — yes."

"Your — clients, or customers, or whatever you call them — members, eh? — are of a superior sort?"

"It really is a dancing club, you know," said Mrs. Emerson. "Dancing is its absolute *raison d'etre.* Yes, the people who come there are of a good sort — they're not the rackety sort you find at night-clubs. I admit no questionable people, under any circumstances. It is, as I say, a club for people who are really fond of dancing and who want to dance."

"Very good! Now, do you know a young lady named Miss Greville — Miss Beatrix Greville?"

"Yes, I know her."

"Is she a regular frequenter of your club?"

"Two or three nights a week — yes."

"Fond of dancing, is she?"

"My belief is that she's been in her time a professional dancer," said Mrs. Emerson. "Yes — you may say she's passionately fond of dancing."

"Well-conducted young woman, Mrs. Emerson?"

"They're all well-conducted young women — and young men, too! — when they're in my club, Mr. Wendover! I see to that!"

"I think you will, Mrs. Emerson! Well, now, my clerk, Mr. Orridge, who invited you to come here, saw, the other night. Miss Greville leave your club in company with a young gentleman who accompanied her in a taxicab as far as the entrance to the flats in which she lives. Can you tell us who he is?"

"Oh, that would be Mr. Sparre — Mr. Bobbie Sparre! He and she are always dancing together — you might call him her dancing partner. Nowadays, these girls who are so gone on the modern style of dancing like to stick to the same partner, you know; yes, that would be Bobbie Sparre."

"And who is Mr. Bobbie Sparre?"

"Oh, just a young man about town! Quite an ordinary, inoffensive sort of youth. Nothing remarkable about him that I know of."

"Do you know of any other gentlemen associated with Miss Greville?"

"I? No! How should I? I only knew her as coming to my club — to dance."

"I mean at your club. Do you know a Mr. Colinrake?"

"No — not at all. He's never been at the Amaryllis — under that name, anyhow! Nobody gets into my club without coming before me. But — what has all this to do with Severfield?"

Bridgwater, who was sitting a little behind Wendover, leaned forward and tapped the solicitor's arm.

"I really think that as Mrs. Emerson has been so frank with us, and as she tells us her sister, who married Severfield, is alive, you should tell her about what we've had reported to us as regards Severfield's intended marriage and his will," he said. "I think she should know."

"Very well," assented Wendover. "Perhaps she should. Mrs. Emerson — the man I mentioned just now, Colinrake, is a solicitor. On Severfield's death being reported, Colinrake came forward and said that Severfield was his client, that Severfield was about to marry a young lady named Beatrix Greville, and that he, Colinrake, had in his possession a recently made will of Severfield's in which everything Severfield possessed was left to Miss Greville. Now do you understand the situation?"

"I've an idea," replied Mrs. Emerson after a pause. "You want to know if everything's all right? I suppose this may have been so! Severfield may have thought my sister was dead — perhaps he did. He never said anything to me of having thought so, though. And he certainly never said a word about marrying anybody else!"

"Well, that's how things stand — and there's no doubt, Mrs. Emerson, that Severfield was murdered! Now, be guided by me. Your sister is Mrs. Severfield. Bring her forward! Get her to come here. There are evidences of foul play — not only as regards Severfield's death, but, I fear, as regards other matters. Let us have Mrs. Severfield to the front! Come! you told me at the beginning that you were a well-experienced woman of the world; I put it to you, knowing all you know now, don't you think your sister should appear?"

Mrs. Emerson rose, as if to leave. She had taken off her gloves; now she slowly drew them on. She was evidently considering the solicitor's last words.

"I cannot promise anything," she said suddenly. "Except this — I will see my sister as soon as possible and tell her of everything that has happened. She must decide!"

She went away then, and, after a little conversation with the others, Credding went off to catch his train. He thought long and hard over the day's revelations as he journeyed to Brighton — thought till his head began to ache, for he foresaw what he called muddle-and-tangle. But before going home he turned in at headquarters. There, just come in, was a telegram from Mrs. Rathbourne.

Chapter XIII
The Six Months' Tenant

Before ever he opened Mrs. Rathbourne's telegram, Credding was aware of an instinctive feeling that he probably held an important clue in his hands. He expected something, anyway — and he was not disappointed when he read the message that had been flashed to him from far-off Bordighera:

Credding. — Police Station, Brighton, England.

"Elvescot" was let by me personally to a Mr. John Taverner, then staying at Beaumanor Hotel, for period of six months dating from August 21st last. No references with him, as he paid six months' rent in advance.

Helen Rathbourne.

Credding put this communication carefully away in his pocket-book. It fulfilled his expectations; it had given him three separate pieces of information. He now knew the name of the tenant of "Elvescot" — John Taverner — and that he was still the tenant, and would be the tenant until the twenty-first day of February in the following year; he knew, too, that when Taverner took the bungalow from Mrs. Rathbourne, he was staying at the Beaumanor Hotel. Excellent! — they would know something about him there, and to the Beaumanor Credding promptly repaired.

The Beaumanor Hotel was one of the smaller, less pretentious houses on the sea-front; the sort of place wherein twenty or thirty guests can be accommodated — all the better, mused Credding, for his purpose; one particular guest would be more likely to be remembered in a small hotel like that than in one of the monster palatial establishments accommodating their hundreds. Credding had a slight acquaintance with the manager of the Beaumanor, one Milledge, and Milledge, on sight of him, and making a shrewd guess that he came' there on professional business, had him into his private room and, as a preface to conversation, produced whisky and cigars. Credding, who had had a hard day's work, refused neither.

"I dropped in to ask you a question or two in connection with my present job," he began, when his glass was at his elbow and his cigar burning well. All between ourselves, of course."

"To do with that affair at Black Rock, I suppose?" suggested Milledge. "I've seen your name in the papers in the accounts of that matter."

"Well, it may have," admitted Credding. "Can't say, of course — yet. But what I want to ask you is, do you remember a man named Taverner staying here, at this hotel, last August?"

"Mr. Taverner? yes, quite well," replied Milledge promptly. "And Mrs. Taverner, too. They were here about a week."

"Where did they come from?" asked Credding.

"That I don't know — can't say off-hand, anyway," answered the manager. "But the register's handy — wait a minute." He left the room, and presently returning with a big book turned its pages over. "There you are," he said. "But no definite address. 'Mr. and Mrs. John Taverner, London.' Merely London."

"And the date?" asked Credding.

"Here from August 15th to August 22nd," replied Milledge. "I remember them leaving. He told me he'd taken a cottage, or something of that sort, Rottingdean way, for the winter."

"I suppose you'd know this man again, if you saw him?" suggested Credding.

"Oh, yes! Tall, rather heavily-built man, black moustache."

"And the lady?"

"Good-looking, florid-complexioned woman. Quiet, decent people. I saw both once or twice, on the front or in the town, after they left here."

"Ever have much talk with him?" asked Credding.

"Oh, nothing much to speak of! Had a drink with him once and again. Not a man to talk much, I should say."

"Have you any idea what his business or profession was?"

"If you ask me, I should say he had some connection with racing," said Milledge. "He was always reading racing news, and buying sporting papers — left a fine old bundle of literature of that sort in their bedroom. That stuff was about all he did read — or the lady either. And he'd a good many telegrams came here of an afternoon — racing results, I took 'em for."

"Did he tell you anything about the place he took for the winter?"

"Nothing — except that he had taken a place. No particulars. They left here in just the ordinary way — settled up one morning after breakfast and drove off with their luggage — couple of portmanteaux."

Credding thought a while in silence. He was not getting much information out of this.

"What's the game, if one may ask?" inquired Milledge.

"Want him?"

"I certainly want to find him!" replied Credding. "I'll tell you why — in strict confidence." He went on to tell the manager just as much as he judged it wise to let him know. "I thought you might have his address, you see," he concluded. "What's down there in your book — London — is no more use to me than if it were Paris or Berlin. But there is one chance — do you know of any Brighton men who ever called to see Taverner here, or in whose company he was ever seen?"

"No," replied Milledge. "I don't know that either he or his wife ever had any visitors while they were here. The fact is, they were very little seen in this hotel. They used to go out soon after breakfast, and he always had a pair of big field-glasses slung round his shoulders. They were never in for lunch. They used to turn in again about an hour before dinner-time at night. He'd collect his telegrams then — I don't remember his having any letters — and sit down in the smoking-room to read them, till the dinner-bell rang — he never changed his clothes for dinner. After dinner they used to go out again and come in late — went to the theatre or the pictures, I guess. That's about all we saw of 'em. They'd one little peculiarity I remember, though," concluded the manager with a laugh. "Don't know if it's any use to you to recall it?"

"You never know what mayn't be of use," replied Credding. "What was it, anyway?"

"Well, from the first night they were here to the last," answered Milledge, "they always had a big bottle of the very best champagne for dinner. Now, as you know, the very best champagne is not cheap, and not easily got. He came to me the first evening he was here and asked what champagne I had in the cellar. I'd plenty, but no brand good enough. He wanted a certain brand, of a certain year, and I said I could get it. He told me to get a dozen bottles — for his use. They'd one every night, and he took the four or five bottles remaining away with him."

"I suppose you deduced from that that he was a well-to-do man?" suggested the detective. "Plenty of money about him just then, anyhow."

"Oh, he'd plenty of money knocking around!" agreed Milledge. "No; what I deduced from that little fact was that he was probably a bookmaker — well-to-do bookmakers have a weakness for champagne. I'm sure he was connected with the turf." Then, as if suggesting an unanswerable argument, Milledge added: "And if that's so, why, you'll have no difficulty whatever in finding him. All these turf chaps are well known to each other. There are some of 'em located here in Brighton; there's" — he went on to mention certain names' all known to Credding — "why not try them?"

Credding replied that he'd bear that bit of advice in mind, and went away, summing up the result of his investigations to that point. Arranged in something like order, they amounted to this:

1. On Monday, October 16th, Martin Severfield came to Brighton, and at shortly after eight o'clock in the evening, in company with Mrs. Emerson, rode in a taxicab as far as the end of Ovingdean Lane, where, the cab having gone away, and he parted from Mrs. Emerson, he turned back in the direction of Brighton, and, consequently, in that of the bungalow called Elvescot, on the beach below which he was found dead next morning, his neck broken and his head having an ugly wound on it that might have been caused by a spanner found near the body.

2. About the time that Severfield — who had told Mrs. Emerson that he had an appointment with a man Rottingdean way — was in the neighbourhood of Elvescot, a man called at a neighbouring garage, and saying that some thing was amiss with his car, close by, bought a second-hand spanner, since identified as that picked up near Severfield's dead body. This man, if the garage proprietor was right in his conclusions, was the man Taverner who had Elvescot on lease from August 21st to February 21st.

3. There appeared to be good grounds for believing that Taverner was the man Severfield spoke of meeting by appointment, and that Elvescot was the place whereat they were to meet.

All the times mentioned during the inquiries fitted in, and there was strong presumption that Severfield was struck down and rendered unconscious at or near the bungalow, dragged across the ground lying between its garden and the coast-line, and flung over the cliffs.

4. The thing to do now was to discover Taverner, and to make certain that he was the man who called at the garage and got the spanner.

5. *But* — Taverner (that is, the man in the car) was accompanied by *a second man.* Who was he?

On further consideration of these things, Credding felt himself undoubtedly worried. Supposing that the man who drove up to, or near to, the garage at the corner of the road leading down to Black Rock, asking for a spanner, really was Taverner — the actual John Taverner who stayed at the Beaumanor Hotel in Brighton from August 15th to August 22nd, and took Elvescot on a six months' lease from August 21st to February 21st — was it anywhere within the bounds of probability that *if* he had an appointment at Elvescot with Severfield, and meant to murder him there, he would openly call at a garage close to which he had lived for a month not very long before? Credding thought it wasn't; he thought it anything but probable. But — there was the undoubted fact that the spanner got from that garage was found near Severfield's body. And — there was also the fact that the garage proprietor was positive that with the man whom he recognised as the tenant of Elvescot there was a second man. Up to now, Credding had not paid much attention to that second man. But at this point he began to realise that the second man was going to be a highly important figure.

After hearing all that Milledge could tell him, Credding, before taking any further steps, decided to have another look round Elvescot, and next morning he went up there and, getting the key from the caretaker, locked himself into the bungalow and proceeded to search it from top to bottom. All he found, of any evident or possible use, was a gilt-edged card, pushed carelessly behind a picture on the mantelpiece of the front bedroom. It was headed *Persimmon Club,* and it informed members thereof that arrangements had been made for the use of an exclusive saloon car on the 10 a.m. train from King's Cross to Doncaster on the forthcoming St. Leger Day: would members desiring to avail themselves of the accommodation communicate with the secretary?

There was no name of any member on this card, nor was the address of the Persimmon Club given. But the finding of the card sent Credding off to London there and then. He had a friend who kept a public-house in the Covent Garden district, and who was well acquainted with sportsmen of all sorts. To him Credding repaired, and in private laid his needs before him, entreating his assistance.

"I know the Persimmon, my boy!" said the friend. "Most of 'em bookmakers that's members there. But this Taverner that you speak of, my boy? — no, he ain't known to me amongst the fraternity."

"Tallish, heavily-built man, with a dark moustache," suggested Credding.

"That description, my boy, would fit a good many!" answered the publican with a smile. "A good many of 'em is tall, and is heavily built, and has dark moustaches. Make it a bit closer, my boy!"

"Can't — that's all I've been supplied with," said Credding.

"Fit hundreds of 'em, that would!" remarked his friend. "Nothing in it, my boy! — that is, nothing to go on. And Taverner, now? — no, I can't call that name to mind — can't remember no Taverner. But — it might be what you fellows call an *alias!* How does that strike you, my boy?"

"Possible!" agreed Credding.

"There is men," continued the publican, with the air of one who communicates remarkable knowledge, 'there is men, my boy, as reg'larly used half a dozen names! Business purposes, in some cases, my boy — all fair and square. Not quite so square in other cases, my boy — see?"

"I see — of course," assented Credding.

"Smith in one place — and to one lot," continued the wise one. "Jones in another — Brown in a third. D'ye take me, my boy?"

"I take you!" said Credding. "Well, now, in this case —"

"I'll tell you what I'll do for you, my boy!" said the publican generously. "You an' me being pals — you leave this little matter to me! On the quiet, d'ye see? What you want to know is — who is, and what is, and where is Mr. John Taverner, as stayed at Brighton part of last August and September? Leave it to me, my boy! — and now, what're you going to have?"

Credding had something — and when he had had it, remembering that he was now in London, he thought that he might as well find out if Wendover had any fresh news, and so bent his steps towards the City. Wendover was engaged when Credding walked into the office, but a clerk took his name in at once, and came back to usher him straight into the solicitor's private room. And there Credding found Bridgwater, and he knew by one glance at the banker's grave and troubled face, that some new and disturbing development had arisen.

Chapter XIV
The Cheque for £ 50,000

Wendover motioned the detective to a chair near his own with a gesture of a man who, in a difficult position, is glad of the advent of anyone likely to advise on it.

"You've dropped in at an opportune moment, Credding," he said. "There's something cropped up in relation to Severfield on which your advice may be useful. But first — anything new yourself?"

"Just a bit," answered Credding. He rapidly summarised his doings and discoveries of the previous night and that morning, down to his visit to the friendly publican. "Of course, I shall get this man Taverner," he concluded. "It's only a question of time."

"Unless — for good reasons — he's removed himself well out of your immediate reach," remarked Wendover. "Don't forget that if Taverner — whoever he may be! — and the man he had with him — whoever he is! — really murdered Severfield, they, of course, had a motive. That motive has probably removed them out of England."

"There were no signs of robbery, you know," said Credding. "Severfield had a good deal on him! Money — jewellery — that diamond ring on his left hand must have been worth a small fortune! And not a thing had been touched."

"No doubt!" observed Wendover, with a dry smile which directed itself towards the banker. "But there may have been other directions in which robbery was effected. In fact, that's just what Mr. Bridgwater and I were busy with when you came in. I'd better explain matters to you. Since Severfield's death, Mr. Bridgwater and his partners, holding, as they do, an immense amount of money belonging to him, have thought it advisable to make a thorough examination of all their books and papers relating to his account at their bank. Everything has been gone through by their clerks — by two very responsible clerks who have taken great care in their investigations — and now Mr. Bridgwater has brought me the results. I've no doubt that if

Severfield hadn't died as he did — suddenly, and under circumstances that seem to indicate murder —"

"Mr. Wendover, there's no doubt that it was murder!" said Credding with emphasis. "None!"

"Very well! Under the circumstances known, then," continued Wendover, "I've no doubt I say, that if he hadn't died under those circumstances there would have been nothing suspicious arising in the results of this investigation. But knowing all that we do know, there's a good deal that's suspicious. Now, when Severfield opened his account at Bridgwater, Manitter, and Bridgwater, he placed to his credit there a very large amount of money. From time to time he paid in further very considerable amounts — it was understood by his bankers that he was selling foreign investments — and placing the proceeds to his credit: his idea, of course, was to re-invest here. Now, from a period of about four months ago, the account shows that from time to time Severfield paid out cheques for large amounts, varying from £ 5,000 to £ 15,000, to Mr. Leicester Colinrake. These cheques were all drawn in favour of Mr. Leicester Colinrake, and came in the usual course to Bridgwater's bank through Mr. Leicester Colinrake's bank. And they may be all in order. Mr. Colinrake may have had this money — it amounts in the aggregate to nearly £ 100,000 — from Severfield for the purpose of investing it for Severfield; if so, Mr. Colinrake will, of course, be able to account for it."

"And suppose he can't?" asked Credding.

"We won't suppose anything of the sort for the present," replied Wendover with a smile. "All the same, you can just bear in mind what I've told you. All this, I repeat, may have been strictly correct — we don't know what transactions took place between Severfield and Colinrake: we hope they were quite proper. Now put that away in your memory and we'll turn to something else — a different affair, and a disquieting one. On the 13th October, three days before he was found dead at Brighton, Severfield called at Bridgwater's bank and asked for and took away with him a parcel of bearer securities the value of which was about £ 30,000. Now here again everything may be all correct, but we don't know what Severfield did with these securities. He had been in the habit of selling similar things himself — he had a box at the bank in which, with his bankers' knowledge, he kept securities — and from time to time he took out certain of them, giving a receipt for what he withdrew. But if he did sell this parcel, he certainly did not pay the proceeds to his credit at the bank. If he didn't sell them, they must be amongst whatever papers and documents he kept at his hotel —"

"Haven't they been examined?" asked Credding.

"Not to our knowledge — so far," replied Wendover. "You've got to remember that Severfield, at the time of his death, was said to have no relations, and that he'd made a will, in Colinrake's possession, leaving everything he had to Miss Greville, and appointing her sole executor. Colinrake informs us that on hearing of Severfield's death, and acting in Miss Greville's interest, he immediately proceeded to the hotel, and, in the presence of a responsible person, sealed up everything of Severfield's which contained or was likely to contain papers and documents, and that he has no intention of breaking those seals, or allowing anybody to break them, until the inquest is over."

"I don't know — as things are — that we, the police, couldn't force him to," said Credding. "I think we could!"

"I dare say you could — by getting an order from the proper authority," agreed Wendover. "But we'll let that pass for the moment. As I've remarked already, this second matter may be all right — the parcel of bearer securities taken away from the bank on October 13th may be found, intact, amongst Severfield's papers at the hotel. Still, put that away in your memory."

"With the first!" assented Credding. "I've got em'!"

"Now we come to the third, and possibly the most important matter," continued Wendover. "On the morning of October 16th, the very day on which Severfield went down to Brighton, there was presented for payment to Bridgwater's Bank, coming to them in the ordinary way through the Richmond branch of the Metropolitan and Mercantile Bank, a cheque for £ 50,000 drawn by Martin Severfield in favour of Mr. J. T. X. Worthington. No question was raised about this cheque; it aroused no suspicion, and it was duly honoured. But now — now! — there is a strong suspicion that the signature is a forgery!"

Credding pursed up his lips to a whistle of astonishment.

"Whew! you're getting to something, gentlemen!" he exclaimed. "Forgery, eh? But — how is it that wasn't detected when the cheque came in?"

"You must remember," said Bridgwater hurriedly, "you must remember that Mr. Severfield had been in the habit of drawing cheques for considerable amounts. There was nothing in the fact that this cheque was for £ 50,000 to arouse suspicion. It appeared, on the face of it, to be perfectly in order, and it was paid."

"Then — why now?" inquired Credding. "Who first suspected it — the genuineness of the signature?"

"One of the two experienced clerks employed to investigate all this," answered Bridgwater.

"What made him suspect it?" asked the detective.

Wendover drew open a drawer in his desk and produced several cheques, which he proceeded to lay side by side on his blotting-pad.

"Here's the cheque in question," he said. "And half a dozen others of Severfield's. Look at them, Credding. Now — do you see any difference between that Worthington cheque and the others? "Credding left his seat and bent over the solicitor's desk. After inspecting the cheques for some minutes he shook his head.

"Hanged if I can see any, Mr. Wendover!" he answered. "There may be. But I shouldn't have said there was. Perhaps they all vary a bit. But me — I should have said they were all written by the same hand. If there is a difference, where is it?"

"I'm not an expert either," replied Wendover. "But I think I see the evidence that Mr. Bridgwater's experienced clerk pointed out."

"And that's — what?" inquired Credding.

"Severfield was evidently the sort of writer who dashes off his signature in a hurry — a rapid, rather scrawly writer. Look at his signature on these six cheques — they all bear out what I've just said. Now look carefully at this Worthington cheque; the signature looks as if it had been slowly written — it's laboured! Look, too, at the short, sharp line, or dash of the pen, underneath the signature. On those six cheques it is just a dash — a quick movement of the pen. On the Worthington cheque it looks to have been slowly drawn. Look at this Worthington cheque from a distance of, say, twelve to eighteen inches, and you see no difference; examine it closely, and I think you do."

Credding looked again at the cheques — and again he shook his head.

"Not for me to say, gentlemen," he said. "I'm no hand at that sort of thing! But who's this Mr. J. T. X. Worthington?"

"That," replied Wendover, "we do not know."

"Not even by name?" inquired Credding.

"Not even by name," answered Bridgwater. "We know nothing about him."

"Never had any other cheques drawn in his favour by Severfield?" suggested Credding.

"Never! The name is quite unknown to us," said Bridgwater. "There are men of that name in the London Directory — many, a great many. But there is no J. T. X. Worthington."

"The 'X.' is a bit unusual," remarked Credding. He picked up the cheque and, turning it over, pointed to the endorsement. "That's the man's writing, of course. Now, I should call that the writing of a man who was no great scholar."

"It is certainly somewhat illiterate," agreed Wendover. "Not what you'd expect in the writing of a man put in possession of fifty thousand pounds!"

The banker made a sound of annoyance; it was plain to Credding that he was much upset about the supposed forgery. And Credding hastened to speak.

"Well, gentlemen," he said. "Why don't you do what I should do at once? That is — run down to Richmond and see the manager of the bank through which this cheque came to yours, Mr. Bridgwater. He'll know who Worthington is! It's still early in the afternoon — you've plenty of time to get along to Richmond before the bank closes. And, if you've no objection, I'll go along with you."

Bridgwater looked at his watch.

"My car will be coming to the bank for me in twenty minutes," he said. "If you both come round there with me, my man shall run us down to Richmond. Of course," he added, giving the detective a dubious glance, "we shall have to be careful about what we say to the man we want to see. It will be best to avoid any references to police action, for instance — at present, at any rate."

"Don't alarm yourself, Mr. Bridgwater," said Credding. "You'll find me a silent partner in this — you and Mr. Wendover can do the talking. All the same," he went on as they set off together, "you're very well aware that, if your suspicions are correct, there'll have to be police action! What I want to know is — does all this hinge on to the murder of Severfield? That's my concern in it; and if I can pick up anything, anywhere, from anybody — well, then, my eyes are as wide open as I can make 'em be! And you never know what luck you may have — in listening."

Three-quarters of an hour later he found himself in a small back-parlour listening intently while Bridgwater explained matters to a branch manager who was obviously somewhat ill at ease, and kept looking from one man to the other as though he were not quite sure of his company.

"That is the position — in secrecy," concluded Bridgwater. "Now if, in secrecy, you'll tell us what you know of this Mr. Worthington —"

The branch manager cleared his throat.

"As far as I know him, or anything about him, Mr. Worthington is a thoroughly respectable man," he answered. "I know nothing to his discredit in any way, Mr. Bridgwater."

"You know him as a customer, of course," said Bridgwater. "Do you mind telling me how long you've known him in that relation?"

"Three years," replied the branch manager promptly.

"What is he?" asked Bridgwater.

"A commission agent."

"What sort of commission agent?" inquired Wendover. "The term is elastic."

"A man of credit?"

"Certainly! In my opinion, if there's something wrong about this cheque you're talking of, I should say that he's quite unaware of it."

"Is he accustomed to pay cheques of that amount into his account?" asked Wendover.

"That — at present — I decline to tell you! He paid in this cheque, anyway, and it was duly honoured without any question or demur at your bank, Mr. Bridgwater. But, if you really want to know more about it than I feel justified at present in telling, why not see Mr. Worthington himself, and ask him your question?"

"That we shall be very glad to do, if we can get his address," said Wendover. "It is precisely what we should wish!"

"I see no reason why I shouldn't give you his address," replied the branch manager. "Mr. Worthington lives here in Richmond. The address is 37, Thamesdale Avenue. I don't know, of course, if you'll find him at home. I have not seen him for several days."

Chapter XV
Forged!

Thamesdale Avenue proved to be a somewhat mean street of cheap red-brick houses, and Number 37 one of those residences the front window of which is invariably decorated with a sickly-looking plant half hidden by more or less dirty white curtains. It was certainly not the sort of house in which one would expect to find a well-to-do man, and the slatternly servant-girl who opened its door to the three inquirers was still less promising.

"Mr. Worthington live here?" demanded Wendover, acting as spokesman. "Is he in?"

"He's not here now, sir," replied the girl; "he's away."

"When will he be in?" asked Wendover. "What time is he in usually?"

Before the girl could reply, a woman appeared from some back region, wiping her hands on her dingy apron.

"Mr. Worthington's away at present," she said, turning an inspecting gaze from one to the other. "I couldn't say when he'll be back. Sometimes he's here, and sometimes he isn't."

"Doesn't he live here — permanently?" asked Wendover. "I was told he did."

"Well, he does and he doesn't," said the woman. "Leastways, he has a couple of rooms here — permanent — for business, d'ye see. He might be here for a few days at a time, and then he might be away a bit."

"You don't know where he is now, eh?" inquired the solicitor.

"No, I'm sure I don't! He was here about a week ago, for a night, but I don't know where he's gone. Did you want to see him?"

"On a business matter — yes," replied Wendover. "I suppose his wife isn't here?"

"I don't know nothing about no Mrs. Worthington," said the woman with a shake of her head. "Never heard her mentioned. I think he's a single gentleman."

"Oh, I see!" said Wendover. "All right-much obliged to you — we'll call again sometime."

"The evening's the best time to see him, when he is here," remarked the woman. "He mostly does his business of an evening. Can I give him any name?"

"No — no! — it's no matter, thank you," answered Wendover. "Some other time." He moved off, followed by Credding and the banker. "What sort of business can it be that's mostly done of an evening?" he asked as they walked back to Bridgwater's car at the end of the street. "Sounds mysterious!"

"Might be a bit of quiet moneylending," suggested Credding. He looked critically at the mean houses. "Poor sort of neighbourhood for a man to live in who deals in fifty-thousand-pound cheques — now and then!"

"He doesn't live here," said Wendover. "I think I see through that! That's a place he uses for business purposes — he may be an agent for some society, benefit, building, assurance. That's the explanation."

"The manager of that branch didn't know of any other address," remarked Bridgwater.

"Probably," assented Wendover. "But that doesn't prove that Worthington hasn't got another! He may have two or three addresses — and two or three banking accounts, too. That cheque just happens to have gone through this particular one."

"I suppose you couldn't have asked that manager if the fifty thousand pounds is still lying to Worthington's credit, Mr. Wendover, could you?" asked Credding. "It would be interesting — and perhaps useful — to know that."

"I could — but he wouldn't have told me," replied Wendover. "I don't think he was very keen about telling us the little he did!"

Bridgwater uttered a sound that denoted a certain amount of surly dissatisfaction.

"I don't like all this!" he said. "I'm sure there's something wrong! What should a man who carries on his business in a miserable street like this, and in a dirty little house like that, be doing with a cheque for fifty thousand pounds? The thing's becoming more and more serious."

"Why not get at a really definite decision about the cheque, then, Mr. Bridgwater?" I asked Credding. "I mean, why not get

116

the leading expert of the day in those matters — handwriting, you know — to examine the cheque and compare it with those other cheques of Severfield's? Then you'd feel satisfied. And what's more, you'd have some ground to go on."

"That's what must be done," said Wendover. "The man to go to is Cannabine. You know his name, Credding?"

"I've heard of him, Mr. Wendover, of course. And I remember that the last time he gave evidence in a prominent case there was a sharp passage-at-arms between him and the judge as to the reliability of his evidence! That particular judge seemed to be very sceptical about experts in handwriting."

"I remember that case, too," said Wendover. "And Cannabine, in the result, proved to be right. Anyway, I think we ought to go to him: I know his address, in Chancery Lane. And if Mr. Bridgwater approves, I propose to go there now, leave all these papers with him, and get him to come to my office to-morrow with his opinion."

"Oh, anything, anything!" said Bridgwater. "The thing must be settled."

"I'll run up in the morning to hear what Cannabine says," remarked Credding. "There's probably more in this matter than's come to the surface yet. And as you're going in that direction, drop me somewhere near Victoria and I'll get down to Brighton."

During the hour he spent in the train Credding reflected on the events of the day. It was very evident from what he had gathered in conversation with Bridgwater that Severfield had had transactions of a financial sort with various people. Was Taverner, the man who had stayed at the Beaumanor Hotel and had afterwards rented Mrs. Rathbourne's bungalow near Black Rock, one of these people? Was Taverner the man of whom Severfield spoke to Mrs. Emerson as the person with whom he had an appointment? The more Credding thought things over, the more he felt certain that Taverner was that man. Yet, if Taverner was that man, why, if Taverner had a design to murder Severfield for some purpose, unguessed at as yet, was he so foolish as to show himself openly at the garage close to the bungalow? Well, the murder might have been one of those unpremeditated affairs, sprung out of a sudden quarrel. Taking it all together, Credding felt certain that Taverner met Severfield at the bungalow on the night of the murder... and as soon as he reached Brighton he went off to the Beaumanor. Hotel once more, having remembered an omitted duty.

Milledge was standing in the hall of the hotel when Credding walked in, and at sight of him beckoned him into the private room in which they had talked before. He closed the door and motioned Credding to a seat.

"I was just thinking of sending round for you," he said. "I've a bit of news for you. About that chap we were discussing the other night — Taverner."

"Well?" asked Credding, alert on the instant. "What?"

"Of course, there were other people in this place when he and his missus were here," said Milledge, "and of course they passed the time of day with some of 'em. Now, one man who was here during that week was a man who comes here fairly regularly throughout the year — a Mr. Gelson, a commercial traveller from Birmingham. I remember seeing him talking to Taverner once or twice when they were both here. Well, Gelson's been in here this evening; he's not stopping here, but he'll be back here in a day or two for two or three days if you want to see him. And he mentioned something about Taverner, quite by chance."

"What?" asked Credding.

"Well, remembering what you'd told me, I took care, cautiously, to find out the exact date on which this happened," continued Milledge. "But, mind you, not until after Gelson had told me what he did tell me. Well, it's just this: on Monday night, the 15th October, Gelson stayed at the Castle Hotel at Newhaven. He'd had a very hard day at his business, and he went to bed early — before ten o'clock. He'd a front bedroom, overlooking the street. While he was undressing there was a sort of noise and commotion going on in the street underneath his window, and he looked out. In front of the hotel there was a motorcar which the two men who were with it evidently couldn't get going — something was wrong with the works. One of the men was Taverner."

"Gelson was sure of that?" asked Credding.

"Oh, certain! Spoke about it chaffingly. He told me as a sort of joke — said if he met Taverner again, he'd pull his leg about his car. They were some time getting it started, Gelson said."

"Did he describe the other man — the man with Taverner?" asked Credding.

"He didn't. Only said there was another man."

Credding sat silently thinking. Newhaven was only a few miles away to the eastward, along the road that passed Elvescot — the times of which he had made a note fitted well together.

"All right," he said. "Much obliged to you. When this Gelson returns, just let me know and I'll have a quiet talk to him. But I came in for another purpose — will you let me see your hotel register?"

Milledge fetched in the book which Credding had seen on his previous visit but had not examined.

"Want to see that entry?" he asked, turning the pages. "Here it is."

Credding bent over the pages and let out an exclamation of disappointment.

"Um!" he said. "A woman's writing!"

"She wrote it," remarked Milledge. "Mrs. Taverner."

"I wanted to see his fist," said Credding. "You haven't got a specimen?"

"No! Don't know that I ever saw his writing," replied Milledge. He closed his book with a snap and gave the detective an arch look. "You're fairly on this chap's back, I suppose?" he suggested. "Want to get hold of him?"

"I should certainly like to be able to put a few questions to him," replied Credding. "He was undoubtedly in this neighbourhood — with another man — on the evening during which Severfield was murdered, and I'd like to know why."

"You'll be coming across him!" said Milledge with a laugh. "It's a small world!"

Credding assented to this platitude and went away to meditate over his supper on the best method of getting hold of Taverner. But there was more than Taverner to be got hold of. There was the second man — Taverner's companion in the car. Who was he? Possibly he, too, was some person known to Severfield; he might be the man with whom Severfield had the appointment mentioned to Mrs. Emerson. But why at that bungalow? No. Taverner must be the man with whom the appointment was

made! Taverner, now that facts had come out, was tenant of Elvescot; he had the keys. Everything pointed to Taverner; the job
was to run Taverner to earth. Meanwhile there was this new development of the cheque — and next morning Credding hurried
off once more to London and to Wendover's office.

An odd-looking little man, carrying a small despatch-case,
was bustling into the outer door of the office as Credding approached it; when, a few minutes later, Credding was shown into
Wendover's private room he found this man there, in company
with the solicitor and Bridgwater. Wendover introduced him —
Mr. Cannabine, the famous expert.

"This is Detective-Sergeant Credding, Mr. Cannabine," he
continued. "He is fully conversant with the affair I put before
you yesterday afternoon. Well? have you come to any conclusion
about it?"

"I have, Mr. Wendover — yes!" replied the expert. "A decided conclusion!" He laid his despatch-case on Wendover's
desk and, taking from it a large envelope, drew out the y various
cheques which Credding had seen the previous day, and arranged
them in order on the blotting-pad.

"Yes!" he repeated, "a decided conclusion! This cheque,
made out in favour of Mr. J. T. X. Worthington by Martin Severfield for fifty thousand pounds, is a forgery! Of that I am assured
— I will stake my professional reputation upon it. A forgery! —
both body and signature! Every written word on it is forged!"

For a moment there was a dead silence in the room. Then
the banker cleared his throat with a sharp, nervous cough.

"I should like to hear some reason for your conclusion, Mr.
Cannabine," he said. "You can give us some, of course?"

"Certainly, Mr. Bridgwater!" replied the expert readily and
cheerfully. "I can, sir! Look at the topmost of these cheques —
we'll call it number one. Now that, according to Mr. Wendover,
is an undoubtedly genuine cheque, actually written by Martin
Severfield on the counter of your bank in the presence of your
cashier, and produced to me as a true specimen of his handwriting and method. I take that as the standard, the criterion, the best.
Now, cheques number two, three, four, five, I affirm to be
genuine; cheque six — the Worthington cheque — a forgery!"

"That's the result of your examination by your own method,
Mr. Cannabine?" asked Wendover.

"It is, Mr. Wendover — but I don't rely entirely on my own method. I have a profound belief in the quantitative method of examining handwriting which really began with Fraser, in America, but was developed splendidly by Locard, of Lyons. I most carefully applied that method to this cheque last night, with the result which I now confidently affirm."

"You'd be able to demonstrate this or to give your proofs of your opinion in a court of law, I suppose, Mr. Cannabine?" asked Bridgwater.

"Oh, to be sure, sir! And to go into all the details. Of course, you know what judges and juries are! — hard to convince sometimes. But," concluded Cannabine, "in this case I am absolutely positive. If that cheque number one is in Severfield's own writing, then this, number six, is a forgery — and, let me tell you — not over a good one, either, in my view! It didn't take me five minutes to see that! But I made a searching and thorough test and examination. Undoubtedly, gentlemen — a forgery!"

Ten minutes later Cannabine went away with his fee in his pocket, and the banker, the solicitor and the detective left alone, relapsed into a grim silence.

Chapter XVI
Cards on the Table

The silence was broken by Bridgwater. He was evidently considerably upset, and during the last few minutes of Cannabine's story had shown signs of growing uneasiness.

"What are we to make of this?" he asked querulously. "Most disturbing! — most annoying! You think his opinion's to be trusted, Wendover?"

"He's the leading man of the day, in his line," replied the solicitor thoughtfully. "I should say his opinion is to be trusted — thoroughly! And, of course, it opens up a big field. These," he continued, pointing to the cheques laid out on his blotting-pad, "are, after all, only a few of the cheques drawn, or purporting to be drawn, by Severfield. There must be many more, and some for large amounts."

"Those for large amounts were, as a rule, drawn in favour of the solicitor, Colinrake," remarked Bridgwater.

"So I understand," assented Wendover, with a certain dryness of tone which did not escape Credding's notice. "So I understand! Well, it may be advisable to have every cheque examined by Cannabine. Now, can you answer this question — did Severfield regularly examine his pass-book?"

"No!" replied Bridgwater. "He did not! As a matter of fact, I was told by my people only yesterday that he'd never had his passbook posted up from the time his account was opened to the time of his death. He had a pass-book given him, or sent to him, when the account was opened, or soon after — perhaps a month after, and my clerks couldn't get it from him again. He was asked for it several times and always took no notice of the request; said any time would do, or something of that sort. He was careless — there's no doubt of it."

"All the more reason, then, why all the cheques should be carefully examined," said Wendover. "I advise you to get them all together, let me have them, and let Cannabine give his opinion on each one. If —"

He was interrupted just then by the entrance of a clerk who came in with a card which Wendover, after glancing at it, laid quietly on his desk.

"Ask him if he will kindly wait a few moments," he said. When the clerk had left the room he turned to his companion with a significant look. "Here is something in the way of a surprise!" he announced. "Colinrake is here!"

The banker looked his astonishment silently; Credding showed his by a sharp whistle. Then he smiled.

"Cool, Mr. Wendover!" he said. "Cool! — cool is the word!"

"I'm certainly surprised," agreed the solicitor. "But we'd better see him. Let him find us together. What do you say, Mr. Bridgwater?"

"Oh, if you think it advisable —" replied Bridgwater testily. "I confess I don't understand it, but —"

"Gentlemen!" interrupted Credding, motioning Wendover to wait. "A moment! Listen to me! Have him in by all means. But, let me urge you strongly not to do certain things! Not one word about Orridge's discoveries concerning Miss Greville. Nor about Mrs. Emerson and the past. Nor about these cheques; put them away, Mr. Wendover, at once, where there's no fear of his seeing them! Not a word about the securities — nor about Worthington! Tell him nothing from our side — nothing! Let him talk if he wants to, as much as ever he likes, but as regards ourselves, gentlemen, the word is — *mum!* Trust me to know the value of my advice!"

"I'm sure you're quite right, Credding," assented Wendover. "Very well! We listen to all and to whatever it is he's got to say, and we hold our tongues. But what's brought him here?"

"Some game of his own, you may be sure!" said Credding. "All the more reason why we shouldn't help him to play it. He may have come," he added, "to find out what game we're playing — I shall soon spot it if he has. But — take my tip, gentlemen — not one word of what we know!"

Wendover rang his bell and bade the clerk who answered it to show in Mr. Colinrake. A moment later Colinrake entered. If he felt any surprise at seeing banker, solicitor and detective closeted together, he showed none. His manner was confident, his bearing polite; he looked like a man who, making an ordinary business call, expects to be met with civility.

"Good morning, Mr. Wendover," he began. "Good morning, Mr. Bridgwater; good morning, Mr. Credding! Gathering of the clans, eh? I certainly didn't expect to find you all together. But perhaps it's as well that I find you here, Credding, for if I hadn't, I should, after seeing Mr. Wendover and Mr. Bridgwater, have run down to Brighton to see you — or your people there."

"Something in our line, Mr. Colinrake?" asked Credding. "Always happy to get a bit of information, you know," he added, with a sly look. "Especially if it's unexpected!"

Colinrake smiled, as if appreciating the detective's humour, and turned to Wendover, who had handed him a chair.

"I've thought it well, Mr. Wendover," he said, "to call on you, as representing Messrs. Bridgwater's bank. It seemed to me that at the opening of the inquest on Mr. Severfield the other day, a line was being taken — not by you, but by the legal representatives of the police, which appeared to reflect I scarcely know what to call it exactly — at any rate, to throw some doubt, or discredit, or something, on the persons affected by Severfield's will —"

"There is only one person affected, is there?" interrupted Wendover. "Miss Greville?"

"Quite so! Well, on Miss Greville, if you like — but, I think, on the will generally," said Colinrake. "Anyway, there seemed to be an attempt on the part of that gentleman to create or to suggest an atmosphere of suspicion. Now I want you to understand — I want Messrs. Bridgwater to understand — I want the police to understand — that whatever may transpire as regards the cause of Severfield's death, everything connected with his will is in strict order — absolutely strict order! And I propose to exhibit the will to you, and to Mr. Bridgwater, and to Credding, as he's present — his presence will save me the trouble of a journey to Brighton."

"I'm no judge of wills, Mr. Colinrake," said Credding with a smile. "I couldn't tell if a will's all right or if it's all wrong!"

"You can, at any rate, stand by and hear what Mr. Wendover has to say," retorted Colinrake. "He'll know a properly executed will when he sees one! And so, I think, will Mr. Bridgwater."

"Do you propose to show us the late Mr. Severfield's will now?" asked Wendover.

"Just now! I have it here in my pocket," replied Colinrake, producing a foolscap envelope. "Here it is! It is not a lengthy document — at Severfield's strict request. It is, as a matter of fact, worded precisely in accordance with his wishes. 'None of your legal verbiage for me, Colinrake!' he said. 'I can say what I want doing with my money in a dozen words. Use the fewest words you can.' Accordingly, the will is short. Now, gentlemen, if you will please to look — there is the will!"

He unfolded and laid on Wendover's desk a single Sheet of stout paper, and the banker and the detective, leaving their chairs, stood on either side of Wendover and looked down at it. And Credding almost immediately gave Wendover a quiet nudge of the elbow. For there, at the foot of the will, put down as witness to its execution, was the signature of J. T. X. Worthington, of 37, Thamesdale Avenue, Richmond, in the County of Surrey, gentleman.

Wendover slightly pressed his shoulder against the detective's elbow as a sign that he had got his warning. For a moment or two he continued to inspect the will. Then he nodded.

"Yes, that appears to be quite in order, Mr. Colinrake," he said quietly. "Quite a model of precise and concise wording! I see that you acted as one witness. Who is the other witness — Mr. Worthington?"

"A friend of Severfield's — often with him," replied Colinrake. "He happened to be with Severfield when Severfield came to my office to sign the will, so he acted as witness with me. Otherwise one of my clerks would have been second witness."

Wendover handed the will back, with a polite bow.

"Yes — as I say — that appears to be all right," he said. "Of course, under the circumstances, you don't propose to proceed to probate just yet?"

"Certainly not!" declared Colinrake. "Not, at any rate, until the inquest is over, and a verdict given. My client. Miss Greville, is anxious that everything should be done in a proper, seemly and above-board fashion. That is why I wished to exhibit the will to you, to Mr. Bridgwater, and to the police. Further, I have this to say. As soon as I received the news of Severfield's death, from Brighton, I proceeded to the Savoy Hotel, and there, in the presence of a responsible person, deputed by the management, I sealed up everything of Severfield's in which papers were deposited' — two trunks, a tin box, and a despatch case. I sealed up another box which he kept at my office. All these seals, of course, are intact. I propose not to open them until the inquest is over or, if it is judged absolutely necessary, to do so on an order from the coroner, in your presence and the presence of a duly accredited representative of the police."

"Very proper, I'm sure, Mr. Colinrake," said Wendover. "Very satisfactory! Mr. Credding will no doubt report what has passed here this morning when he returns to Brighton, and the police authorities there will, if they think it necessary, communicate with the coroner."

"Oh, yes!" said Credding. "I'll report to my people. Of course, what we're concerned about is — who murdered Severfield?"

Colinrake was putting the will away in his pocket. He buttoned his overcoat across his chest, and picked up his hat and umbrella. Then he gave the detective a look.

"So you think Severfield was murdered, do you, Credding?" he said.

"Don't you, Mr. Colinrake?" asked the detective, with an air of simplicity.

"No!" said Colinrake. "Not he! He fell over the cliff!"

"What about the medical evidence?" suggested Credding. "The doctors —"

"Pooh!" exclaimed Colinrake. "I dare say you could have found other doctors who'd have flatly contradicted those who were called. Even they weren't certain. No — the verdict will be death by misadventure. Good morning, gentlemen!"

Colinrake went away as suddenly as he had come, and Credding, after inspecting the faces of his companions, wagged his head knowingly.

"Bluff!" he said. "All bluff! That chap's playing a game! Now, what game is it?"

The other men regarded Credding inquisitively; evidently there was something in the detective instinct that was natural to him which was not clear to their own perception.

"You think he has a game?" inquired the solicitor.

"Think!" exclaimed Credding contemptuously. "I don't think — not much, Mr. Wendover! Why, put it to yourselves, gentlemen! We know the circumstances under which Severfield came to his end — at least, we know a good deal about them. Whatever Colinrake may say, Severfield was murdered — and the verdict of the coroner's jury will be one of murder — and, I hope, not against some person or persons unknown! Well, now then, we find that one of the witnesses to Severfield's will is a man named Worthington — J. T. X. Worthington, and don't you forget the combination of initials, J. T. X. — said, by Colinrake, to be a friend of Severfield's. Now Colinrake doesn't know it, but we already knew something about J. T. X. Worthington before we saw his signature on Severfield's will just now. We'd seen that signature before! And where? As the endorsement of a cheque purporting to be made out by Severfield to J. T. X. Worthington — which cheque, according to the opinion of the foremost expert of the day, is — a forgery! Game? I should say it is a game!"

"Extraordinarily suspicious!" muttered Bridgwater. "Yet the will" — he broke off, looking at Wendover — "you considered the will all right?"

Credding spoke before the solicitor could answer this question.

"Look here, gentlemen!" he said. "You listen to me! I'm no lawyer — I wouldn't presume to contradict one. But — Mr. Wendover isn't an expert in handwriting, either. Cannabine says that £ 50,000 cheque is a forgery: how do we know that the will isn't a forgery? The man who could forge that cheque could forge that will — see?"

"That's what's in your mind, is it, Credding?" said Wendover. "Of course, if Cannabine could have examined the will —"

"Cannabine, sir, will have the opportunity!" declared Credding with emphasis. "We — the police — will have something to say about that will, now that I know all I do about the cheque. 'The cheque, and Cannabine's report about it, brings all this within our province. That will, gentlemen, may be all right — but it's got to be inquired into! So have other matters."

"Such as — what?" asked Wendover.

"Well, now, there's those securities — that parcel of securities that Mr. Bridgwater says Severfield personally took away from the bank just before his death," answered the detective. "That parcel may be found amongst Severfield's papers at his hotel, which, according to Colinrake, are sealed up — and don't you forget, gentlemen, that even if they are all sealed up, Colinrake had access to all of them before he sealed them up — what?"

"You suspect Colinrake?"suggested Bridgwater.

"I think it a queer thing, Mr. Bridgwater, that a man should be murdered very soon after making a will in favour of a young woman of — eh? — somewhat doubtful character!" replied Credding. "I suspect all sorts of things in connection with this case. The first thing now, in my opinion, is to find this man J. T. X. Worthington — I'll see about that; I shall probably have to go to Scotland Yard about it, and get some assistance. But there's a thing you can do, Mr. Wendover. Put that clerk of yours, Orridge, on to keeping an eye on Miss Greville; let him find out if she's seeing Colinrake, if she's being visited by Colinrake — and tell him to be careful not to arouse any suspicion on their part. This is an intricate problem, gentlemen — but we shall solve it!"

Then Credding went away, and it being already well past his usual dinner-hour, he sought out a comfortable restaurant and took his time over his food and drink and his after-dinner cigar. He meditated, too — and his meditations eventually sent him, later in the afternoon, once more to Richmond.

Chapter XVII
The Barber's Shop

The instinct that led Credding back to Richmond was a good deal akin to that which sends an intelligent terrier to a likely place for rats. He had no particular plan; he might be going on a wild-goose chase; whatever he did might end in failure — but something impelled him to go, and he went. He knew, of course, that he wanted to find the man J. T. X. Worthington; if he couldn't find him in person, he wanted to find out something about him. He had no definite ideas as to this finding, but long experience had taught Credding that if you keep eyes and ears open you often make a happy discovery when you least expect it; anyway, a few hours' prowling around the district in which Worthington undoubtedly lived at times, and had an address well known to his bankers, might yield handsome profit.

Instinct, again, led Credding, in the gathering dusk of the autumn afternoon, to the neighbourhood of Thamesdale Avenue. And there, at the corner of that respectable but eminently dull and mean street, he noticed a barber's shop — one of those establishments in which two trades are combined, the owner figuring as tobacconist in front and hairdresser in the rear. Now Credding knew that if there is any place in which news may be picked up cheaply and readily it is a hairdressing and shaving saloon; there the gossip of the neighbourhood is more easily learnt than in even the bar-parlour of the inn. He took off his hat and ran a hand over his hair — well, it would do with a trim, anyway, and as the place looked clean, and he might pick up a bit of information, he entered.

The barber was disengaged and reading the early edition of the evening paper. He installed Credding in a chair and talked about the weather. Credding led him skilfully from the weather to the healthiness or otherwise of the district; from the district in general to Thamesdale Avenue in particular; the barber gathered from Credding's remarks that he was interested in house property, and he proceeded to inform his customer as to the rents, sizes, arrangements, and general capacities of the houses, with the front door of one of which, at any rate, Credding was already acquainted. And Credding might have led him to a mention of Number 37 if, while the barber was putting the finishing touches to him, the door of the saloon had not opened to admit a man.

Credding had a big mirror in front of him. He could see this fresh customer in the mirror. He was a big, broadly built man, clean shaven. He Wore a smart overcoat, a smart, rather rakish hat; he carried a gold-mounted umbrella in one hand; a morocco-leather suit-case in the other. He nodded to the barber, set down his suit-case on a chair, leaned his umbrella against it and, removing his hat and overcoat? showed himself in a fashionably-cut suit of dark tweed, set off by a tie which in Credding's opinion was designed to show either racing or club colours. Then he picked up the paper which the barber had laid aside at Credding's entrance, and dropped heavily into a chair.

The next instant Credding knew his luck. His pulses bounded as the barber spoke, and his ears pricked. But he kept a straight and unconcerned face.

"Fine evening, Mr. Worthington," said the barber. "Improving, don't it?"

"Can't say — been away of late," answered the big man in a deep voice of which Credding immediately made a mental note.

"Thought I hadn't seen you lately," remarked the barber. "Far away, Mr. Worthington?"

"Paris," replied the other laconically.

"Ah! And how was gay Paree looking, Mr. Worthington?"

"Just as it always does!" said Worthington. "Pretty much like any other place."

"Ain't never been across myself," remarked the barber. "There was a pal o' mine, he wanted me to go, one time — Pricks de Paree, you know, Mr. Worthington — but it didn't come off — wife was a bit off-colour, or something."

The man addressed made no comment on this piece of news, and the barber, removing the wrapper from Credding with a flourish and an "I thank you!" adjusted the rest at the back of his chair in readiness for shaving. And Credding, having been brushed, paid his money and went out, highly elated. Without a doubt, the big man now succeeding him in the barber's chair was the man he wanted.

It was dark now, and Credding was glad of it. He stepped quietly across the street and posted himself in a convenient place from which he could keep an eye on the door he had just left. Twenty minutes went by — Worthington was evidently having a thorough doing-up at the hands of the barber. But he came out at last, suit-case and umbrella in hand, and marched off towards Number 37. And Credding followed, at a safe distance, congratulating himself on the fact that Worthington, because of i his height and bulk, was a very easy man to keep in sight, the sort of quarry that you could pursue safely in either Cheapside or the Strand, where crowds are thick. There was no need to hurry after him, or to keep at his heels — still, the detective, when Worthington arrived at Number 37, was near enough to his man to see him admit himself at the front door by means of a latchkey.

Once more Credding posted himself in a convenient position to watch. He saw a light suddenly appear in the window of the front parlour of the house; he saw Worthington in the room; he saw the woman whom he had seen before when he and Bridgwater and Wendover had called there, come into the room, and Worthington turn to her; he saw her cross to the window. She drew down the blind — but before she did that the detective had just time to see Worthington tearing open the envelope of a letter which he had evidently found on the table.

It was fortunate for Credding that the street was badly lighted and that he stood on the opposite side in a patch of dark shadow, for within two minutes of the blind's fall across the window, Worthington came hurrying out of the door. He had neither umbrella nor suit-case now, and it seemed to Credding from the momentary glimpse he got of his face in the light of the nearest lamp that he looked excited or upset. That he was anxious to get somewhere or to somebody in as quick a time as possible was evident; he set off at a rapid pace by the way he had come, and Credding had to put his best foot foremost to keep him in sight. The end of Thamesdale Avenue at which the barber's shop stood abutted on a street which led into a main thoroughfare that ran to the heart of the town. Worthington traversed all three. And Credding never losing sight of him, felt no surprise when at last Worthington reached the Metropolitan and Mercantile Bank and rang the bell of the private door. The detective had already realised what had happened at Number 37.

Worthington had found a letter from the branch manager telling him about the call there of Bridgwater and his companion; the landlady had doubtless told him they had been there, too. And now Worthington was seeking the bank manager — for information.

Once more Credding resigned himself to waiting. That was a busy and crowded street, and it was an easy thing to post oneself right in front of the bank and to watch the private door without fear of being seen or suspected. And this time he had to wait longer — half an hour, three-quarters. Then Worthington suddenly appeared on the step, and with him the bank manager, hatless.

For a few moments these two men, in whom Credding now took an immense interest, remained talking — in the detective's opinion, in great confidence: it was quite evident, anyway, that they were on unusually friendly terms. Eventually they shook hands with much cordiality, exchanging smiles and nods in the process; then the bank manager went into his house and closed his door, and Worthington hurried down the steps to the pavement. And once more he set off at a round pace, but not in the direction of Thamesdale Avenue. This time he made towards the District Railway station, and Credding, following him more closely, was so near to him when he reached the booking-office that he heard him ask for a ticket to Charing Cross. A moment later Credding got a ticket too, and when Worthington presently boarded a City train, the detective was close at hand.

Credding was close at hand again, all unknown to his quarry, when Worthington left the train at Charing Cross. He followed Worthington along subways and passages to the Tube: he tracked him to Piccadilly Circus; when Worthington got out at Piccadilly Circus, Credding got out too, and feeling secure in the fact that Worthington wouldn't know him from Adam, he went up in the same elevator. Worthington was obviously preoccupied; he never looked at anybody in the elevator, which, as usual, was crowded; he looked neither to right nor left when he stepped out. What he did was to hurry away across the Circus, and into Shaftesbury Avenue, and Credding was close on his heels all the time.

Half-way up Shaftesbury Avenue Worthington turned sharply into the open door of a range of flats; by the time the detective reached that door he had disappeared up the stairs. Credding strolled slowly past, keeping his eye cocked on the important side. And as he passed, he quickly noted one or two facts — first, that there was no hall-porter visible; second, that there was no sign of any lift; third, that on the wall just inside the entrance there was a board on which in black letters appeared a list of names — flatholders, of course. And twisting in his tracks, Credding slipped inside that hall, and within two seconds had slipped back into the street. But he had seen what he expected to see, and that was the name of

Mr. L. Colinrake, Second Floor.

Credding went slowly along the street, and twenty yards farther up, crossed it, and coming back on the opposite side, posted himself right in front of the door from which he had just emerged. While he stood there, waiting and watchful, he thought. Things were going very much as he had expected they would go after seeing Worthington hurry from his lodgings to his bank. He had seen the bank manager, and now he wanted to see Colinrake. Credding began to speculate. Would Worthington and Colinrake, in conjunction, want to see somebody else, a third party? One thing was sure — Worthington, whoever he might be, was a familiar of Colinrake's. The detective began putting things together: the forged cheque — Worthington's signature as witness to the Severfield will — the hurried flight from Thamesdale Avenue on hearing of the Bridgwater-Wendover-Credding visit — the call at the bank manager's private house — now the call on Colinrake at his private flat; it all meant something. And — what next?

The next was the sudden appearance of Worthington in the hall opposite. There he was! — but Colinrake was with him, and though Credding knew that he was safe from recognition, he instinctively drew farther back and away. But he never took his eyes off the two men, and when they came out and walked up their side of Shaftesbury Avenue, Credding followed, at a proper distance, on his.

Up to this point all Worthington's movements, when alone, had been hurried. But those of Worthington and Colinrake together were leisurely. They strolled along at a gentle pace, as though they had no particular object or mission, and Credding had no difficulty in keeping them in sight while he himself hung well in the background. But there was evidently a purpose in their walk, for they kept going ahead, and always in the Bloomsbury direction. And eventually they led Credding to the entrance of the flats called Madresfield Mansions, and he remembered then that this was where Miss Beatrix Greville lived and the scene of Orridge's operations in connection with his investigations.

Worthington and Colinrake entered Madresfield Mansions and so were lost to sight, and Credding, after a cautious inspection of that entrance, decided that he would have to exercise more care here than at the Shaftesbury Avenue flats. The Madresfield Mansions entrance was an imposing affair — there was an outer hall and an inner hall, and he could see a hall-porter and a lift-boy. Obviously it would not do for him to shove his nose inside. So once more he had to betake himself to the opposite side of the street, and to seek a convenient patch of shadow between the lamps, and to wait — for what, and for how long, he didn't attempt to guess.

Luckily he had not to wait long. Within ten minutes the two men appeared again, and again they walked slowly away, still talking earnestly. Credding followed, as a matter of course — by that time he was prepared to follow anywhere until something happened. But suddenly his men got away from him. A taxicab swung round a corner, its flag up; before Credding had time to realise it, Worthington and Colinrake had stopped the driver, given him an order, jumped inside the cab, and were retreating in the distance.

That was in a quiet street, where there was no other cab in sight and no cab-stand near. Credding accepted the situation with equanimity and walked quietly on until he came to the lights of a tavern. Reflecting that he had now been several hours on the prowl without refreshment, he turned into the saloon bar, and retreating to a corner with a whisky and soda, drew out his little pocket-book, intending to post it up while things were fresh in his memory. And turning over its recent pages his eye was attracted by an entry: *Amaryllis Club, Hallam Street.*

Something impelled Credding to go there and then and have a look at this establishment — from the outside, anyway He had already decided to stay the night in London, so that he could see Wendover first thing in the morning and tell him of his discovery of Worthington; he might as well devote another hour before turning into an hotel to making an inspection of the Amaryllis Club. This, he remembered, was about the time at which, according to Orridge, its members began to assemble. And presently, having emptied his glass and lighted his pipe, Credding went out once more, and finding a taxicab close by, bade its driver to take him to the corner of Hallam Street and set him down there.

But before Credding's cab got as far as that corner he suddenly found out where Worthington and Colinrake had gone when they got away from him. As his cab crossed Portland Place, another, coming swiftly from the opposite direction, shot past — but not too quickly for Credding to see its occupants, whose faces were shown clearly to him in the strong light of a centre street-lamp. There were three people in that cab: he knew them all — Colinrake, Worthington and Miss Greville. And they were all talking excitedly.

The detective let his cab go on. He had a notion. When he got out of it at the corner of Hallam Street, he walked slowly along, keeping his eyes open for the place he wanted, and at last finding it, went up to the porter at its entrance and asked for Mrs. Emerson.

Chapter XVIII
Mrs. Emerson's Room

The janitor of the Amaryllis Club was a very large man in a very grand semi-military uniform; from beneath the peak of his gold-braided cap he looked down on the detective with calm inquiry. And deciding that he had not come there to dance nor to flirt nor to look on at both or either, he vouchsafed one questioning word:

"Business?"

"Exactly — business!" replied Credding.

"Sees nobody on business at this hour," said the porter. "Business hours ten to one of a morning — no other time."

He turned away unconcernedly, as if Credding had been sufficiently crushed. But Credding walked after him, and drawing out his pocket-book, produced and thrust a professional card before him.

"See here, my man!" he said. "You take that to Mrs. Emerson, just now! She'll see me — on my business!"

The porter looked, stared, and after another glance at the detective, opened a side door in the handsomely-appointed entrance hall and vanished within. In less than two minutes he was back.

"See you in a few minutes," he whispered. "Of course, you see, I didn't know who you was — what? And she's that partic'lar about anybody being admitted. Take a chair."

Credding took a chair, a comfortable, beautifully-padded easy chair, and gave himself up to watching. Somewhere within the building a string band was playing dreamy music; in the entrance hall itself men and women, just arrived, were chatting and laughing; every now and then cabs rolled up to the outer door and set down more seekers after pleasure. They were all eminently respectable-looking folk, even if they were, without exception, garbed in the very height of fashion, thought Credding, and he remembered Mrs. Emerson's boast that her establishment was conducted on irreproachable lines.

Presently, when the throng in the inner hall was thinning, a young man in evening dress, his fur-collared overcoat thrown wide open, a cigarette between his lips, and what Credding set down as a general air of refined degeneracy about him, strolled carelessly in. He nodded to the porter, glanced at a clock on the mantelpiece, and going up to the fire, threw his cigarette into the flames and proceeded to draw off his gloves and warm his hands. Suddenly he turned to the porter.

"Miss Greville come yet?" he asked in a dull, colourless voice.

"Come and gone, Mr. Sparre," replied the porter unconcernedly.

Credding thought he saw a slight flush of colour in the young man's otherwise unusually pale cheek; he thought, too, that he saw him start.

"What d'ye mean — gone?" he demanded.

"What I say, Mr. Sparre. She came in about her usual time, and she was talking to another young lady here for a minute or two. Then two gentlemen came for her —"

"Who?" asked Sparre quickly.

"I don't know! Nobody that comes here. She went away with them, there and then — one of 'em tall, darkish man, came in for a minute; the other was in the lobby there. They went off in a taxi that the gentlemen had come in. Ten or fifteen minutes ago, that is."

Sparre made no answer. He drew out a cigarette-case and began to smoke again, staring thoughtfully at the pattern of the thick carpet. Suddenly he looked sharply at the porter.

"Leave any word — any message for me?" he asked.

"No, sir — nothing! In a hurry, I think — somebody dead, I should say. The gentleman who came in, he was in a hurry."

Again Sparre relapsed into silence, studying the carpet. Once more he suddenly looked up from it, buttoned his overcoat, and with a curt nod to the porter, strode out, to vanish in the street. The porter, left along with Credding, gave him a confidential wink.

"Pipped!" he said. "Young lady missing! Bit of a jealous young gentleman — "

Before Credding could hear more, or reply fittingly, a door opened, and a young woman who wore spectacles and carried a bundle of papers in her hand came out and looked inquiringly about her.

"Mr. Credding?" she asked.

Credding rose and went forward; the young woman pushed the door wider open; Credding walked into a smartly-furnished but eminently businesslike room, in the centre of which, at a desk, her attitude as businesslike as her room, sat Mrs. Emerson. She nodded to the detective as the door closed behind him, motioned him to a chair at the side of her desk, and twisted her own round to face him.

"Yes, Mr. Credding?" she asked. "What is it?"

Credding smiled as he sat down and unbuttoned his overcoat — a signal on his part that there he was and there he meant to stay until he had discharged his mission.

"More than can be told in a few words, Mrs. Emerson!" he answered. "Certain things have happened that have forced me to the conclusion that my best policy, if I want to solve the mystery of Severfield's murder, is to come and see you, and — I may as well say at once — make a confidante of you. That's about it, ma'am."

"Why me?" asked Mrs. Emerson.

"You'll see, before I've gone far," replied the detective. "There are reasons — and good ones! But now, Mrs. Emerson, before I say anything, will you, in view of all that talk at Wendover's office the other day, give me a plain answer to a plain question?"

"Probably!" said Mrs. Emerson. "What is it?"

"That sister of yours, Mrs. Emerson — is she alive?" asked Credding. "That's the plain question!"

"Yes!" said Mrs. Emerson. "She is! That's your plain answer."

"And producible?" demanded Credding. "Available? Close at hand?"

"She's in London," replied Mrs. Emerson.

"And still — legally — Mrs. Severfield?" asked Credding eagerly.

"Oh, certainly, certainly!" said Mrs. Emerson. "Yes!"

"Very well, ma'am — much obliged to you," continued Credding. "Now, if you'll listen carefully to me, I'll just tell you what I want you to know as a preparation to asking you to do something. It's a longish story, but I'll do my best — though I'm no lawyer, you know! — to make it a clear one."

Mrs. Emerson listened closely while Credding went on to tell her all that he himself knew and had learned, and had found out about the Severfield matter from the time he was put in charge of it until that evening. She was a good listener — he saw that; she appreciated points — he saw that, too; certain features of the case, he felt, struck her far more forcibly than they had struck either Wendover or Bridgwater. And when he had finished, she spoke promptly and definitely.

"Your notion, as a detective, is just this, isn't it?" she said. "You believe, in view of all these facts, that there has been forgery, and possibly theft, and eventually murder, and that both Colinrake and this other man Worthington are mixed up in all three — and possibly the murderers? That it?"

"I think they know the secret about the murder," said Credding. "I think — now! — that probably either Worthington or Colinrake was the man who was with Taverner in the car seen outside Welford's Garage when Taverner went there and got the spanner from Welford."

"You haven't traced Taverner?"

"No — but I'm doing my best. I shall get him — unless, indeed, he's left the country already. As I say — I think it may have been Worthington, or it may have been Colinrake, who was in that car along with Taverner. There may have been a gang — all three members of it!"

"You suspect Colinrake of actual guilt, or complicity?"

"Mrs. Emerson, I'll tell you what I suspect!, I suspect that will! In my opinion, it'll be found out to be a forgery — like the fifty-thousand-pound cheque. I haven't said so yet to either Mr. Bridgwater or Mr. Wendover, but that's my firm belief. Everything, in my opinion, points to this — that these men, or they and some others or other in collusion with them, devised plans for getting hold of Severfield's money by getting rid of him. I've told you what I've seen with my own eyes to-night! Colinrake and Worthington together — here, at your your place — to fetch that girl, hurriedly! Why?''

"Do you think the girl's an accomplice?" suggested Mrs. Emerson.

"I should say the girl's a cat's-paw! I saw and heard her in the witness-box when the inquest was opened, and I couldn't make her out. But, I imagine, more of a cat's-paw, an instrument, than an accomplice. She's in it somehow, anyway."

"What do you want me to do, Mr. Credding?"

"This! Produce your sister, Mrs. Severfield! And — at once! Now — can it be done?"

Mrs. Emerson considered this direct question in silence for a while.

"What effect would that have?" she asked at last. "I mean — as regards what you're doing?"

"It's my belief it would bring matters to a crisis," answered Credding. "According to what I've understood from Mr. Wendover, your sister, as widow, could interfere with this alleged will, don't you see? Then the authenticity of the will in existence would be gone into. And if it's found to be a forgery — why, then, there's good ground for suspecting Colinrake and whoever's concerned with him of getting rid of Severfield so that the forgery could be brought forward as a genuine document! Do you see?"

"That's what has been done already," remarked Mrs. Emerson.

"Precisely! But the will in Colinrake's hands has up to now been taken as genuine! Now, if it's found out that it isn't — then we shall have a fine case! Anyway, Mrs. Emerson, get your sister to come forward!"

Mrs. Emerson thought a little more. Suddenly she looked up and gave Credding a nod.

"Very well!" she said. "I will! I'll bring her myself to Mr. Wendover's office at twelve o'clock to-morrow morning. That's definite. You'll be there?"

"I'll be there!" answered Credding.

He went away after that, greatly elated by the success of his visit. It was getting late then, but he still felt disposed to further efforts, and Madresfield Mansions being close to the hotel at which he proposed to pass the night, he took a walk in that direction — why, he scarcely knew; it was hardly likely that he would see any more of Colinrake, or of Worthington, or of Miss Greville at that time. He did not expect to see them; but as he turned the corner of Madresfield Mansions he saw, walking up and down outside the front entrance, the young man whom he had seen in the inner hall of the Amaryllis Club, and whom he had heard the porter address as Mr. Sparre.

Sparre had his back to Credding and was loafing about with bent head, and Credding, recognising him on the instant, contrived to shoot across the street and into a patch of black shadow before Sparre turned again. When Sparre turned, it was to walk back; to turn again, to walk back again; evidently he was keeping watch. And there being a dark entry between two houses close by, Credding slipped into it out of his shadow, and continued to watch. For Sparre was obviously waiting, and not only waiting, but determined to wait for somebody — that somebody could only be Miss Greville.

Ten minutes — twenty — half an hour went by; then, with a gesture of impatience, Sparre turned sharply from the pavement and, running up the steps, pushed open the swing doors of the flats and went inside. Then he disappeared from Credding's view; but Credding continued to wait. And after some minutes had elapsed, Sparre came out again — and this time, walking rapidly, he went round the corner and vanished, and Credding felt instinctively that he had gone for good. Thereat he went off to his hotel, and during an hour's meditation over a glass and a pipe he came to certain conclusions which, as soon as he had breakfasted next morning, took him off to Scotland Yard, where he was quickly closeted with a great man in close deliberation.

When Credding left Scotland Yard, at ten o'clock, it was in the company of another man of his own profession, a Detective-Sergeant Rollinson, detailed to aid him in certain proceedings on which, in consultation with the great man, he had decided to take. Credding put Rollinson into a taxicab, and sped down to 37, Thamesdale Avenue, Richmond, there to inquire for Mr. J. T. X. Worthington. But Mr. Worthington was not there.

"Which he was here, for a few minutes, latish yesterday afternoon," said the landlady, answering the detective's knock in person. "He come in, from being away, and there was a letter for him, and I told him as how you and them other two gentlemen had called to see him, and he went out there and then, and he ain't never been back since. Can I give him any message?"

Credding thought not and, motioning the cabman to follow him and his companion up the street, he led Rollinson in the direction of the barber's shop at the corner.

"I'm not going near that bank manager yet," he said. "Of course, he'll know a good deal about the disposition of that fifty thousand pounds, and he'll have to tell, in the end, how it's been disposed of. But we'll leave him alone at present, till we know more; there's a man here that we may be able to get a bit of information from as regards Worthington's habits when he's at these lodgings — anyway, he knows him."

The barber was unoccupied. He recognised Credding at once. And when Credding, with an air of great secrecy, had whispered in his ear just as much as he thought it sufficient for him to know and had introduced his companion as a famous Scotland Yard man, his whole spirit rose to the occasion, and his interest became as keen as one of his own razors.

"Well, now, you know, gentlemen, I always did consider him a bit of a mystery man!" he remarked. "So did others around this quarter. Never knew what his job was. He'd be here — at Number 37 down the street — for a few days, then he'd be off. Nobody here ever knew what he did. And I can tell you something that I thought queer!"

"What's that?" demanded Credding.

"Well," replied the barber, "he used to wear a black moustache — a well-trimmed one. About ten days or so ago — just before he went across to Paris — he shaved it clean off, himself!"

Chapter XIX
The Surprise Theory

The barber imparted this piece of information as if it were of the utmost value; he winked and nodded as he gave it, thereby implying that there was more in the news than perhaps struck the ear. But the two detectives, true to professional tradition, affected not to be surprised.

"Ah!" said Credding. "That struck you, did it? Thought it a bit queer, eh?"

"Well, a man don't shave his moustache off for nothing — in my opinion," answered the barber. "Now, he'd a good, carefully-looked-after moustache, he had — the sort of ornament that some men would have been proud of, see? But — off it comes! And — all of a sudden!"

"Make much difference to his appearance?" inquired Credding.

"I believe you! Scarcely knew him when he come in next time! — had to look at him hard. Oh, yes — it changed him."

"And that was just before he went away to Paris, eh?"

"Well, of course, I didn't know he was going to Paris — not till he'd been and had come back — you was in the shop when he come in that night, and you heard what he said. It was before he went away — come in one afternoon with it shaved off. I passed a remark about it — he said he'd taken a fancy to be clean-shaved; thought it suited his style better. But I dunno!"

Credding and his companion went away and, re-entering their taxicab, drove to the City, to Wendover's office. Wendover listened eagerly to all that Credding had to tell of his recent adventures. He made no comment on any feature of them save one.

"You say Mrs. Emerson promised you she would call here to-day, and bring her sister, Mrs. Severfield, with her?" he said. "That's definite?"

"Definite!" replied Credding. "She'll be here at noon. Fixed it herself."

"It's now half-past eleven," remarked Wendover. "I'll telephone to Mr. Bridgwater and get him round. But now, Credding," he went on, after ringing up the banker and getting his answer; "what are you going to do when this interview with the two ladies is over — I mean as regards these men, who are evidently in some collusion in this matter?"

Credding glanced at his companion.

"Scotland Yard's in at this now, you know, Mr. Wendover," he answered. "I posted them fully in all the facts of the case this morning. What are we going to do? Why, I suppose, get on the track of both Colinrake and Worthington, and, when we've come across them, ask them a few polite questions."

"What do you mean by 'on the track'?" asked Wendover. "Do you suggest they've run away?"

"Not yet, I think," said Credding. "No — I mean we'll call at Colinrake's — and, if he isn't there, we'll find him. And we'll find Worthington — and perhaps we'll give Miss Greville a call at her flat. Preliminary inquiries, you know, Mr. Wendover — just to see what we can pick up. But a good deal depends, of course, on what we hear from this lady — Mrs. Severfield. I suppose she'll have some power to step in?"

"Oh, decidedly!" replied Wendover. "As long as we find that she's the lawful wife and widow of Severfield — undoubtedly. But after hearing all you've told me about your last night's doings, I think I should suggest that you get in touch with those men as quickly as possible. Now, supposing you do — this afternoon — and suppose Worthington, for example, refuses to say anything to you about that cheque — what then?"

"We shall just invite him — politely but firmly — to go with us to Scotland Yard, and give an explanation about it there," answered Credding. "We're going on what the expert — Cannabine — says: that the cheque's forged. Very well! what has Mr. Worthington to say about that? Oh, we'll turn him inside out, once we get him, Mr. Wendover — leave that to us!"

Bridgwater came in just then. He was not alone; there came with him an elderly, smartly dressed man whose deeply bronzed face and grizzled moustache gave him a military appearance, and who looked round him out of a monocled eye with obvious interest and curiosity.

"My solicitor, Mr. Wendover," said the banker. "Wendover, this is Colonel Penkridge, who had called on me just before you rang me up — to give me some information about this Severfield affair. He had seen your advertisement in *The Times* and, having met me previously some time ago, he came to me this morning instead of to you. And now he'd better tell you what he has to tell."

"Very pleased to hear it. Colonel Penkridge," said Wendover. He turned towards the two detectives. "So, I'm sure, will these two police-officers — Detective-Sergeant Credding, Detective-Sergeant Rollinson. Any information — —"

"I don't know that it is information, Mr. Wendover," said the Colonel, taking the chair which Credding drew forward. "What I have to tell is more in the way of a suggestion. I saw your advertisement in the South of France. I've only just returned, or I should have called on you or on Mr. Bridgwater sooner. I called on Mr. Bridgwater this morning, instead of on you, because I remembered meeting him once or twice at a friend's house here in London some little time ago. Well, I've already told Mr. Bridgwater what I know, and I gather from him that there is no doubt that the Martin Severfield who was found dead under suspicious circumstances at Brighton is the Martin Severfield who, some years ago — twenty or twenty-one or-two years ago — had a sheep station in Australia — New South Wales?"

"No doubt whatever. Colonel," replied Wendover. "That's established!"

"Then I think there may be something — perhaps a good deal — in what I can tell you," continued Colonel Penkridge.

He glanced smilingly at the detectives. "I dare say you gentlemen have already progressed pretty far in this case?" he said. "Got a theory of your own, no doubt! Now, if your theory isn't working out quite as you like, or expect, may I ask if another idea has ever struck you — that Severfield was murdered by some man who wanted to have his revenge on him for an old wrong?"

Rollinson looked at Credding: Credding slowly shook his head.

"No evidence before us to suggest that, sir," he answered. "None!"

The Colonel looked at Bridgwater and then at Wendover and smiled. But the smile ended at Credding.

"Are you quite certain of that?" he asked. "Mr. Bridgwater has summarised for me the facts of this affair as far as it's gone, and he tells me that soon after Severfield's death, in consequence of the advertisement to which I've just alluded, a Mr. Marsland came here, and gave Mr. Wendover and Mr. Bridgwater certain information as regards Severfield's life on his sheep station in New South Wales. I believe you, the police, are in possession of that information?"

"We are, sir," replied Credding. "All of it!"

"But evidently you didn't attach much importance to, or follow up, one feature of it," observed Colonel Penkridge, with another smile. "Now, do you remember that Mr. Marsland, in the course of his story, said that when young Mrs. Severfield and her sister. Miss May — who now, I hear, is a Mrs. Emerson — ran away from Severfield's place in his absence, and Severfield, re-turning home, went after them, a man — a young man — came there, inquiring for the two young ladies?"

"That's in my recollection, sir," agreed Credding.

"Very well, that's what I'm going to tell Mr. Wendover and you two all about," said the Colonel. "There may be something in it — there mayn't! But in view of what's happened, it's well worth considering. Now, to begin with — some twenty-two years ago, when I had already been a few years in the Army, my medical advisers discovered that I was likely to develop very serious chest trouble. I didn't want to give up my profession, and, to make the story short, matters were so arranged that I was able, on the advice of the doctors, to go out to Australia for twelve months. I came back, I'm glad to say, a perfectly sound man. Well, most of my twelve months in Australia were spent in Sydney. Like most young fellows of my age, I was fond of amusements and a constant frequenter of the theatre and the mu-sic-hall. There were two young ladies came to Sydney — I think from Melbourne — while I was there: the Sisters Maybury. They, I needn't tell you, were the two sisters you have heard of in connection with Severfield. They were pretty, attractive, lively girls, well educated, and they were run after a good deal by the young men. That's an undoubted fact! Now there was a young fellow in Sydney at that time, evidently possessed of ample means, whose name was Stephen Dalmer —"

"A moment, if you please, sir," interrupted Credding, producing his little notebook. "I'll write that down — how is the surname spelt, now?"

"Dalmer," replied the Colonel. "He pronounced it as if it were written Dawmer. He was an Englishman — I've an idea that he, too, had gone out there for his health. Well, this young Dalmer, there is no doubt, was madly in love with the younger of these two girls — her name was Rhona. He was always dancing attendance on her; always sending her presents — flowers, sweets, perhaps more expensive things. Whether she encouraged him or not, I can't say. Matters certainly seemed to be progressing when Severfield came on the scene. I knew Severfield well enough at that time; he joined a club — or was, perhaps, already a member of it — to which both Dalmer and myself belonged. I believe it was Dalmer who first took Severfield to the music-hall at which the two girls were appearing; it was certainly Dalmer who introduced him to them personally. Severfield became infatuated with the younger girl — and unfortunately for Dalmer, he, Dalmer, was just then obliged to go off to Melbourne on some business which he couldn't neglect. I have no doubt you already see what happened. During Dalmer's absence Severfield persuaded the girl to marry him, and he at once carried on her and her sister to his sheep-station."

Colonel Penkridge paused for a moment, and Wendover put in a quiet question.

"I suppose there's no doubt about the marriage?" he asked.

"Oh, none, none!" replied the Colonel. "No doubt whatever! As a matter of fact, I acted as Severfield's best man. They were married at St. Andrew's Cathedral. It was a hurried affair; Severfield, as I remember him, was the sort of man who had the power of persuading people to do things — a forceful, masterful man. Well, there it was! He'd got the girl and carried her off, and her sister with her — their contract at the music-hall was just over. We at the club, of course, knew there would be ructions when Dalmer returned. Some time elapsed — he was still away, and I learnt afterwards that on his arrival at Melbourne he'd found it absolutely necessary to go to Ceylon, to see a brother — who was a tea-planter there — on some important family matters. But he came back, and, of course, heard what had happened. The girl, evidently, had not informed him by letter or otherwise of her decision between him and Severfield. Well, Dalmer took it badly — very badly! And if you want the bare truth, he swore a most awful oath in my presence and that of another man that if he ever came across Severfield he would kill him at sight — whether it was next day, or next year, or twenty years hence! And I may tell you that Dalmer was one of those men in whom the desire of revenge for a wrong done is not likely to die out. Of course, we expostulated with him, tried to calm him down, laughed at him; he said nothing. And, for the time being, he did nothing. I don't know that he even asked for Severfield's address. But he once said to me, quietly, that if ever he met Severfield, that moment would be Severfield's last, for, he added, Severfield had betrayed him."

"A strong motive!" remarked Wendover.

"Precisely — especially in this particular man's case," agreed Colonel Penkridge. "Now, I left Australia just after that, and I heard no more of any of these people. But after hearing from Mr. Bridgwater the story which Mr. Marsland told, I have no doubt whatever that the man who came to Severfield's sheep-station inquiring for the two girls, after they had run away, was Dalmer. And I am very sure as to what would have happened if he had met Severfield! His resentment and anger when I knew him were of the quality that is not likely to die out or even to die down!"

Wendover nodded, and turned to the detectives.

"What do you think of all this?" he asked, looking at Credding. "That is, in view of all we know?"

Credding, who had made more notes in his book, closed it, and restoring it to his pocket, shook his head,

"In view of all we know, Mr. Wendover," he answered, "I don't think there's anything we can act on in Colonel Penkridge's suggestion. You see, sir," he continued, turning to the Colonel, "there's no doubt of this: Severfield, on the night of the murder, was lured into a bungalow called Elvescot, near Black Rock, and either there or in its grounds, or on the cliff close by, was struck down by a spanner which was found near the body."

"You're quite sure of those facts?" asked Colonel Penkridge.

"I am!" declared Credding. "It's what I'm going on. Now, supposing this Dalmer is still alive, and is still — or was — of revengeful intent, what would he know about this bungalow, and so on? And — I know where the spanner was got!"

"Also," remarked Rollinson, backing up his colleague, "we know the man who got it — though we haven't got him yet!"

"In that case," said Colonel Penkridge, smiling, "your task seems —"

Wendover's head clerk entered the room and whispered to him. Wendover whispered back, and when the clerk had gone, turned to his companions.

"This is something of a dramatic moment!" he said. "Here are the two ladies you have spoken of, Colonel — Mrs. Emerson and Mrs. Severfield!"

The five pairs of eyes were bent on the reopened door. Mrs. Emerson, businesslike as usual, appeared; behind her, shrinking timidly came a woman in what seemed to be the garb of a nun.

Chapter XX
Who was the Other Man?

Whatever embarrassment her sister felt about stepping into a room full of strange men, Mrs. Emerson showed none. She came forward with a general nod and smile, addressing herself to Wendover. And she plunged straight into business.

"Now, Mr. Wendover!" she said, with easy familiarity of a woman of affairs. "Here I am, in pursuance of my promise to Mr. Credding, and here is my sister, Mrs. Severfield! No doubt you're surprised to see her in that — costume, we'll call it. The fact is, Mr. Wendover, when my sister and I came back to England twenty years ago, she became a member of a certain nursing sisterhood that's well known in the poorer parts of the East End, and she's been in it ever since, and as a matter of fact she's now its Superior. Hence, what you see!"

"We are very glad to see Mrs. Severfield," answered Wendover, in his politest manner. He drew forward chairs for his visitors; then suddenly motioned Mrs. Emerson towards Colonel Penkridge. "Here is a gentleman, Mrs. Emerson, whom I believe you were once acquainted with."

Mrs. Emerson started and stared as the Colonel came forward. Then she smiled and held out a hand.

"Goodness!" she exclaimed. "Johnnie Penkridge! After all these years! And now, I suppose, Mr. Wendover has heard still more about those doings in Australia?"

"Something more, Mrs. Emerson," replied Wendover. He waited while Penkridge shook hands and exchanged a few words with the two sisters. "Just enough," he continued, when they had all settled down, "to enable me to be in a position to put a few questions to your sister, if she'll be kind enough to answer them."

"My sister, Mr. Wendover, is here to answer any questions you like to put to her," replied Mrs. Emerson. "I've posted her up in everything that I know about this affair, and put the situation fairly before her. She'd far rather answer your questions than go into a witness-box."

Wendover secretly thought it extremely unlikely that Mrs. Severfield would be able to avoid the contingency of which her sister spoke, but he kept his thoughts to himself.

"I don't think we shall trouble Mrs. Severfield with many questions," he said. "You can soon tell me what it's really important that I should know, Mrs. Severfield — and I gather that you're aware, through Mrs. Emerson, that I am pretty well acquainted with certain events in the past. Now, to begin with, you were Miss Rhona May — that was your real name?"

Credding was watching the quiet figure in the sombre garb with a keen inquisitiveness. Mrs. Severfield, he could see, had been a very pretty woman —-was still one, in his opinion. But she was of a different type to her sister, and he was not surprised that her brief answer to Wendover's question came in shy and timid accents.

"Yes," she said. "That was my name."

"And you married Mr. Martin Severfield at St. Andrew's Cathedral, in Sydney?"

"Yes!"

"I believe this gentleman. Colonel Penkridge, was present?"

"Yes, I remember Colonel Penkridge being there, very well."

"Just so. Now, Mrs. Severfield, have you kept — that is, if you had it — what is commonly called the marriage lines — a certificate?"

"Yes! I have it here — I have always kept it," replied Mrs. Severfield, producing an envelope. "You will find it in there."

Wendover glanced the document over and turned to Bridgwater and Credding.

"This is extremely fortunate!" he remarked. "It will simplify matters immensely. Now, Mrs. Severfield, without going into painful matters, I take it that your marriage was a great mistake and you — in short, you left your husband, came back to England and joined your sisterhood?"

"Yes!"

"Been in the sisterhood ever since, I suppose?"

"Continuously."

"Well, you know what has happened to Mr. Severfield. You know, too, I suppose, that a man who professes to have acted as his solicitor has a will of Severfield's which he claims is in order, but about which we are now doubtful. You must come forward, Mrs. Severfield! You have rights. The whole thing must be gone into."

Mrs. Severfield made no answer for a moment or two. She sat looking down at her hands. Finally she shook her head.

"I don't want to come forward," she answered at last. "I — I would prefer, if you please, that there should be no publicity. And — and I don't want Mr. Severfield's money, if that is what you mean."

"What I mean, Mrs. Severfield," said Wendover, "is that you should at any rate give your help towards preventing the success of what may turn out to be a gigantic and particularly shameful fraud! And as regards your not wanting the money, just let me put something to you. I know your sisterhood by name, well enough — everybody does! I dare say Mr. Bridgwater has given plenty of subscriptions to it, and I know what good work it does in our East End. Now, even if you don't want this money for yourself, think how immensely useful it would be to your sisterhood! You could make vast use of it — you could, for instance, build and endow a hospital!"

Mrs. Severfield smiled, for the first time since entering the room. She let the smile go round the men watching her steadily.

"That would be very nice!" she said. "Very nice indeed! We should certainly be glad of that."

"Well, we shall see what can be done," replied Wendover. "Now that we know you are there, and what you can prove, we shall take immediate steps to prevent this alleged will being proved, and so on. You need have no compunction about taking Severfield's money if we can get it for you — that is, I mean, such share of it as you're entitled to; for, if we upset this will, that will mean that Severfield died intestate, and you'll get one half the personal property and the Crown will get the other half, while as regards any real property, you'll get one-third, and the Crown the rest — for it seems quite certain that he has no other relations; no one has come forward, anyway. For the present, leave all that to me — I'll look after your interests. But now, arriving out of a conversation we've had with Colonel Penkridge this morning, I want to ask you a question or two about another matter — and a not very pleasant one. I suppose, Mrs. Severfield, you have a very good recollection of your stay in Sydney, about the time you were married to Mr. Severfield?"

"I remember a good deal."

"I believe you had other admirers than Severfield, hadn't you?"

"I — I think there were others," admitted Mrs. Severfield shyly.

"No doubt!" said Wendover gallantly. "Now, do you remember one in particular — a Mr. Stephen Dalmer?"

"Yes. I remember him quite well."

"Will you tell me this — had he asked you to marry him before Severfield did?"

"Yes, he had!"

"Had you given him any encouragement?"

"No — I was afraid of him. He had a very violent temper. I never gave him any encouragement — never promised anything."

"But perhaps he was of the sort that won't take no for an answer?"

"He was very persistent, certainly!"

"After Mr. Severfield came on the scene?"

"Yes, I think so — as far as I recollect."

"And you married Mr. Severfield, rather suddenly, during Dalmer's temporary absence?"

"It was sudden, yes. And Mr. Dalmer had gone away."

"Well, now, Mrs. Severfield, I want you, if you please, to answer this: since you left Australia, have you ever heard of Mr. Dalmer?"

The men sitting round and watching Mrs. Severfield saw her face change colour. But she confronted Wendover candidly.

"Yes!" she replied. "I have. I have never told anybody of it — not even my sister — until now. But there is nothing to conceal about it. About three — or perhaps four — years ago, I saw an advertisement in the personal column of *The Times,* asking me — it referred to me as Rhona Maybury, my old stage name — to communicate with Stephen Dalmer. The advertisement appeared several times. I took no notice of it."

"Was any address given?"

"No; any reply was to be sent to the office of *The Times.* As I have just said, I made no reply. And — perhaps I had better tell you, now that you have brought up his name — I have seen Stephen Dalmer."

"Seen him! Where, Mrs. Severfield?"

"It was at Brighton. Walking on the front. I knew him at once."

"When was this?"

"Two years ago. We took a number of children from Poplar down to Brighton for the day — I was in charge of the party. I was with some of the children on the front when I saw Stephen Dalmer coming along. I think I noticed him first because he had two very fine dogs — mastiffs — with him; they attracted the children's attention. I recognised him."

"Did he know you?"

"No, I am sure he did not. Indeed, as soon as I saw him and had assured myself that it was he, I took care that he should not know me. I turned away until he had gone by."

Wendover glanced at Credding. And Credding, who was sitting in a shadowy part of the room, made a signal to the solicitor which Wendover took to mean that in the detective's opinion enough had been said. Wendover acted on it.

"Well!" he said, "I think that's all, Mrs. Severfield. Please leave all this in my hands. I'll see to your interests. And we won't bother you any more than we can help. I know, of course, where you are to be found. Now look forward to that hospital you would like to build!"

Presently the two sisters went away, and Wendover, after watching them to the door, looked round on his companions. Colonel Penkridge spoke.

"I'm very glad you didn't tell her that Dalmer threatened Severfield's life!" he said. "Considering what's happened, and that Dalmer's alive, and in Brighton, that would have been — trying to her!"

"That Dalmer is alive and in Brighton — or was, when she saw him — raises a very serious question," said Wendover. "If it's possible for a man to harbour feelings of revenge —"

"Twenty years!" muttered Bridgwater.

"Twenty years!" exclaimed Penkridge. "Pooh! I've known men who harboured revenge longer than that — and gratified it in at least one instance! And Dalmer was a black-tempered chap!"

Credding suddenly spoke.

"Gentlemen!" he said, "I know that man! Not by the name of Dalmer, though — not by any name. I knew him as soon as she, Mrs. Severfield, mentioned the dogs — mastiffs. He's a man who lives in Brighton; I've known him for some time by sight: he always has these two dogs out with him. Pedigree dogs, I should say. Well! I can soon get hold of him! But — that spanner!"

"You've got that spanner fixed firmly in your mind, Credding!" said Wendover good-humouredly.

"That spanner, sir, I'll stake anything, is the weapon with which Severfield was stunned previous to his being thrown over the cliffs!" declared the detective doggedly. "How else could it come to be found where it was?"

Wendover made no reply to this. He was standing with his back to the fire, watching the detective. Suddenly he smiled.

"Credding!" he said, "that you've worked hard at this case I've no doubt! — you have. But there's a certain man mixed up in it as to whom I can't recollect your saying a single word!"

"What man, Mr. Wendover?" demanded Credding.

"The man who was in the car outside Welford's garage when its owner got that spanner from Welford! The second man! Who was he? — who was the other man? You're pretty certain, by this time, that the man who got the spanner was Taverner, tenant of Elvescot, and probably you'll lay hands on Taverner, sooner or later. But who was Taverner's companion?"

Credding nodded and sat silent for a while, in evident reflection.

"It seemed to me," he said at last, "that the thing to do was to get hold of Taverner first. Indeed, the only thing I could do! I'm hoping to get definite news of Taverner here in London, from a man in the know; you see, I have some clue to Taverner: I'm sure to get him! But now I'm off to Brighton, next train, to see this man with the mastiffs — Dalmer. Rollinson, there's a matter you can attend to. Find out, cautiously, if Colinrake's at his office — get to know anything you can about him. We shall have to follow up this business about Colinrake, Worthington and the girl — we'll get at something along one side track or another. Mr. Wendover! Where is that clerk of yours Orridge?"

Wendover laughed.

"I have no idea, Credding!" he replied. "Orridge has carte blanche! But I should say that Orridge is after Colinrake — pursuing his own methods!"

Chapter XXI
Luck

Credding hurried off to catch the next fast train to Brighton: for the twentieth time since this affair had cropped up he thanked his stars that London and its virtual suburb by the sea are so closely linked up; it seemed to him that he spent half his days running from one to the other. And during this particular hour's run he meditated on what he had just learned — Mrs. Severfield had certainly given him something new to think about. He knew the man with the mastiffs well enough by sight: he was a well-known Brighton figure. A middle-aged, hard-bitten, sporty-looking sort of man, reflected Credding: smartly dressed, apparently well-to-do; he had seen him many a time with his dogs, here and there about the town, at odd times during the last two or three years. And though he didn't know his name before, he had no doubt he knew it now — it was not likely that there would be two men in Brighton who led mastiffs about, and as for the address, that would be easily got, if this man still called himself Stephen Dalmer. They had an up-to-date directory at the police-station; he hastened there as soon as he reached the town — to have a telegram thrust into his hand.

The telegram was from the friendly publican of Covent Garden whom he had asked to help him in respect of Taverner. A mere word or two:

Some news for you if you will call.

Credding thrust the message into his pocket and turned to the local directory. The name he wanted to find was an uncommon one. And he saw it at once — the only instance of its use in all the town.

Dalmer, Stephen, gentleman, 2a, Kenilworth Mansions.

Close at hand! Kenilworth Mansions stood within two minutes' walk. Credding put the book back in its place and reflected. Should he first make some inquiries about this man? Should he get another detective to go with him to the address given? He threw both notions aside: he would call on Dalmer himself, and at once. Five minutes later he rang Dalmer's bell.

Credding's summons was answered by a smart-looking youth who seemed to be something between a valet and a page-boy. Credding, following out a line of conduct and procedure which he had carefully, though quickly, decided on, inquired if Mr. Dalmer was at home, and finding that he was, presented his professional card with a request for an interview. "Within a couple of minutes he found himself bidden to enter Mr. Dalmer's flat, and shown into what was evidently its dining-room.

"Mr. Dalmer will see you in a few minutes, sir," said the youth.

Left alone, Credding looked about him, and quickly decided that Mr. Stephen Dalmer was interested in sport, and particularly in horse-racing. Over his mantelpiece there was a fine oil painting of a famous Derby winner; old racing and hunting prints decorated the walls; the sideboard displayed several silver cups, and a bookcase in a recess by the fire was filled with books about racing, hunting, shooting and the like. There was a general air of well-to-do-ness about the room; not likely, thought Credding, that he would find a murderer in its owner.

The door opened suddenly to admit Dalmer, in whom Credding at once recognised the man with the mastiffs. He saw at a glance that Dalmer was probably about the same age as, Colonel Penkridge; perhaps not quite so well preserved. Distinctly a sporty-looking man and, evidently, approachable. He had the detective's card in his hand and smiled as he looked from it to its presenter.

"Yes?" he said inquiringly, as he closed the door and came forward. "Want to see me?"

"If you'll be so good as to give me a few minutes, Mr. Dalmer," replied the detective. "Shan't detain you long."

Dalmer pointed to a chair near the fire, and took one, opposite, himself.

"Yes?" he asked.

"Not a very pleasant matter that I've come about," began Credding. "I'll go straight to the point. As you're a Brighton resident, Mr. Dalmer —"

"Not permanent," interrupted Dalmer." I spend my time between this and London, where I have another flat. Sometimes here, sometimes there."

"Well, semi-resident, then," continued Credding. "Anyway, I dare say you are aware of the recent affair at Black Rock — the death, and probably by murder, of Mr. Martin Severfield?"

"Yes!" replied Dalmer promptly. "Read all about it — as much as there's been — in the papers, of course. I wasn't here at the time, though. I was away in the North, shooting in Durham and Northumberland, until the end of October."

Credding silently reflected that that bit of news settled matters as regards any possibility of Dalmer's guilt or participation.

"You weren't here — in town — when it happened?" he said.

"Scarcely! — considering that I was three or four hundred miles away!" replied Dalmer. "I came here nearly a fortnight later, not so many days ago. But why?"

"I believe you knew the late Mr. Severfield?" said Credding.

Dalmer smiled.

"Well, I did know him — years ago!" he answered. "Oh, yes! Now how do you know that I knew him?"

"I heard it from two people," replied Credding. "One, Colonel Penkridge — whom, I think, you knew at the same time, in Australia; the other, Mrs. Severfield, who was formerly Miss Rhona Maybury."

Dalmer's brows had contracted to something like a puzzled expression at the mention of Penkridge; when Mrs. Severfield's name was mentioned he stared keenly at his visitor.

"Maybury — or May," added Credding. "You knew her, too, I think?"

"Where is Mrs. Severfield?" asked Dalmer sharply.

"Mrs. Severfield, sir, has for a great many years been a member of a religious community, working in the East End of London," replied Credding. "She's now the — I don't know what they'd call it — she's the boss, anyway, Mr. Dalmer. But, of course, though she calls herself Sister Something-or-other, she's legally Mrs. Severfield."

Dalmer looked his astonishment.

"Where did you come across her?" he asked.

"Oh, in the course of my inquiries, Mr. Dalmer. And Colonel Penkridge in the same way."

"I remember him now," said Dalmer. "Johnnie Penkridge! Army chap — out there for his health. Um! That's years ago — must be twenty, at least."

"Twenty-one or two, Mr. Dalmer. These people remembered all the events there well enough."

"And — they mentioned my name to you?"

"They did, sir! Your name is an uncommon one. I put two-and-two together. And as you knew Severfield in those days at Sydney, I called to ask you if you'd ever seen him since — and particularly if you'd ever met him since he came to England nine months ago?"

"I've never seen Severfield since I knew him in Australia," replied Dalmer. "Nor heard of him until I heard of his death. I guessed of course, when I read about him in the papers, that he was the man I'd known out there; afterwards I found, from what came out, that he certainly was the man. No! — I've never set eyes on Severfield for all these years. I'd almost forgotten him. Once upon a time, if we'd met, there would have been a row — perhaps worse!"

"Yes?" said Credding invitingly. "Severfield," continued Dalmer, "played me the dirtiest trick one man can play on another! When I first knew him, I was all but engaged to be married to the lady you've just referred to. I introduced Severfield to her and her sister, and, from that on, he was always in attendance on them. He told me he was after the sister; that was a lie! — he was after my girl. I had to leave Sydney on most urgent business at Melbourne; when I got to Melbourne, I was obliged to travel there and then to Ceylon, and I was accordingly away from Australia for some weeks. When I got back, I found that Severfield had married my girl and carried off her and her sister to his place up-country! That, as they say nowadays, is that!"

"Nasty," said Credding sympathetically.

"It hit me!" Dalmer went on. "Badly! I've some faint recollection that I swore an oath or something that I'd shoot Severfield on sight — I was young and silly then. However, the thing was done — he'd got her. But I very soon guessed that all wasn't well — that the marriage was a mistake."

"How was that, Mr. Dalmer?" inquired Credding.

"This way. Some time after I'd returned to Sydney from Colombo, I got a letter from the sister which aroused my suspicions. She enclosed a cheque on an English bank, signed by herself and her sister — in their stage names, mind you! — and asked me to get it cashed for her in Sydney and to send her the money to the post office in a certain town, which, on consulting a map, I made out to be some little distance from Severfield's sheep-station. Now that letter had come to Sydney in my absence; it had been sent on to Melbourne; it had followed me to Ceylon; it had been sent back from my brother's place in Ceylon to my Sydney address; consequently it was weeks and weeks old! However, as soon as I got it, I got the cheque cashed, and I set off to carry the money myself. I got to Severfield's place — an out-of-the-way spot it was, too! — only to hear that Mrs. Severfield and her sister had gone away, and that Severfield was off, too. And never hearing anything more of them, I sent the money to the bank in England on which the cheque had been drawn, explaining the circumstances. Of course, my opinion has always been that the girls wanted that money to run away with! — and that when they didn't hear from me, they got funds elsewhere. However. that's all done with! And so Mrs. Severfield is a — what? Sister of Mercy? — bless me!"

"That's it, sir," said Credding. "And if she gets Severfield's money, or whatever share she's entitled to, she's going to build a hospital, or something of that sort. Well — I'm much obliged to you, Mr. Dalmer!"

"Quite welcome!" answered Dalmer. "Sorry I can't give you any information. I believe, from what I've read in the papers, that you police incline to the opinion that Severfield was murdered?"

"Oh, undoubtedly, Mr. Dalmer, undoubtediy!" replied Credding. "I've never had any doubts about that, myself, from the first."

"Making any progress?" asked Dalmer.

"Some — in various directions," answered Credding. "There are no end of queer complications — loose ends — sidetracks. I shall piece things together bit by bit, I feel sure."

"I didn't read the account of the opening of the inquest," remarked Dalmer. "I was away then. But I noticed that when the inquest was resumed the other day, it was immediately adjourned again, without any further evidence being given."

"It was, sir, at our request — at the request of the police," assented Credding. "We were not in a position to go on."

"Do you suspect anybody?" inquired Dalmer.

Credding smiled, shaking his head.

"Hard to say, Mr. Dalmer, hard to say!" he answered. "You know, in a case of this sort, there are usually several people that you *could* suspect! But suspicion's not proof, nor even evidence. One muddles on — finding out this, then that, then t'other; I've been on half a dozen different trails already — I'm on most of them now — jig-saw puzzle work. Now, I see," continued Credding, nodding at the pictures on Dalmer's walls, "I see you're a racing man. There's a man I very much want to find in connection with this Severfield case, who I believe, from what I've gathered, has or may have something to do with the Turf. I wonder, seeing that you evidently favour racing, if you've ever heard of or come across him? His name is Taverner — John Taverner."

The next instant Credding knew that luck had come his way! — good luck, the best of luck! — and all by chance, mere chance. Dalmer's face lighted up.

"Taverner?" he answered. "Oh, yes, I know Taverner — Jack Taverner! What about him?"

"What is he?" asked Credding eagerly.

"Oh, a sort of commission agent. Sometimes, too, he does a bit of bookmaking. Buys and sells horses, too, at times. Various irons in the fire, I should say. And I have a notion that he does a little quiet financial work."

"Do you know where he lives?" demanded Credding.

"No — if you mean his private address. I saw him once or twice here in Brighton at the end of last summer — he told me he was renting a cottage somewhere just outside."

"He was!" said Credding with a grim smile. "But I wish I knew where he lives — when he's at home — or where I could come across him!"

"Well, I do know this," remarked Dalmer. "He's a member of the Persimmon Club, and of the Craiganour Club, too, I fancy. But, then, he's another name that he's known by, you know — like a lot of these fellows."

"What name?" asked Credding.

"Worthington," replied Dalmer. "J. T. X. Worthington. His name's John Taverner Xavier Worthington — his real name.

Some times he's Taverner for business purposes. But — what's the matter?"

For Credding was giving pantomimic expression to his feelings and indulging in strange motions and ejaculations.

"Matter, sir?" he exclaimed. "The matter is, Mr. Dalmer, that by mere chance I've hit on the very thing I wanted to know! I'll tell you more later, sir — good afternoon."'

Then Credding rushed out, and after hastily telephoning to Wendover in the City, and to Rollinson at Scotland Yard, he ran, faster than was good for him, to catch the 5.35 from Brighton to Victoria.

Chapter XXII
The Italian Restaurant

When Credding arrived at Victoria, it was to find both Rollinson and Wendover awaiting him outside the barrier, and it immediately struck him that each had news. He hurried them off to a waiting-room and got them into a quiet corner.

"Anything happened since I left you this morning?" he asked.

"We were just discussing that when your train came in," replied Wendover. "Yes! Mr. Bridgwater came to tell me, this afternoon, that as a result of certain inquiries they've been making in the City, they've found that the parcel of bearer securities which, you remember, Severfield personally took away from the bank just before his death was sold, some days — a good many days — ago. And — by Colinrake!"

"Well, that's just what I expected, Mr. Wendover!" said Credding. "What else? Of course Colinrake had the run of Severfield's rooms at the hotel after his death! I always believed that Colinrake would collar all he could lay hands on. And I suppose those securities were worth a lot?"

"A very substantial amount," assented Wendover.

"And he'll have got it in cash, now, of course!" remarked Credding. He turned to Rollinson. "What about Colinrake?" he asked. "Been to his office?"

"He's never been near his office all day," replied Rollinson. "I went there — made an excuse. His clerk says he didn't turn up this morning, and he's never heard from him. I called at the flats he lives in, in Shaftesbury Avenue, too. The caretaker there says he saw him go out last night with a man whose face was familiar to him through having seen it now and then, but whose name he doesn't know, and since then he hadn't returned."

Credding made an exclamation expressing disgust and annoyance.

"Colinrake's off!" he said. "I ought to have stopped those two — and the girl — last night! But then — I was on foot, and they were in a taxi, and going quickly. And I'd no help, and if I had stopped 'em I couldn't have detained them on what I then knew. But now! — well, there's the plain fact — Colinrake's got the start of us — unless that clerk of yours is after him, Mr. Wendover. Do you think he is?"

"I've neither heard nor seen anything of Orridge for some days," replied Wendover, "and that's a pretty sure indication that Orridge is busy. He was told to keep an eye on Colinrake and on Miss Greville, and he's sure to carry out his instructions."

"I saw nothing of him, hanging about last night, though," remarked Credding. "Still, he no doubt has his own methods."

"He certainly wouldn't follow the methods of anybody else!" said Wendover with a smile. "I think you may take it that Orridge is up to something."

"Let's hope so!" said Credding. "Well — I've news, too. I've seen this man Stephen Dalmer that Colonel Penkridge and Mrs. Severfield told us of."

"You have!" exclaimed Wendover. "Quick work!"

"Oh, easy job, that! I told you I knew him by sight — from her description. He turned out to live within two minutes' walk of our head-quarters. I went straight to his flat and saw him. He remembered all about the doings of twenty years ago in Sydney. Said Severfield cheated him out of the girl, but laughed over the idea of the threat he made in Penkridge's presence. Knew nothing about Severfield except what he'd read in the papers. Was away in the North of England, shooting — Durham or Northumberland — at the time of Severfield's murder. I soon saw that Dalmer had nothing to do with that! Got nothing about it out of him. But I did get the most useful bit of information I've got in the whole course of this inquiry — a perfect godsend of luck."

"And that is — what?" asked Wendover.

Credding chuckled, looking from one man to the other.

"Ah!" he said delightedly. "What do you think? Came unexpectedly — and was as welcome as a fortune would be to a pauper! Listen! Taverner, the tenant of 'Elvescot,' the man who got the spanner at the garage near Black Rock, the man who was all about there, without a doubt, on the night of the murder — Taverner is... Worthington! What do you think of that, now?"

"An *alias?*" suggested Wendover.

"Whatever you please to call it, Mr. Wendover! That's the fact! Worthington and Taverner are one and the same man. This

Mr. Dalmer knows him. He's a bit of all sorts of things — chiefly connected with the Turf. Sometimes he calls himself Worthington — that is his proper name: John Taverner Xavier Worthington — sometimes he's Taverner. Oh, yes! — Dalmer knew him quite well."

Wendover drew a long breath.

"That's serious, Credding!" he said after a pause. "That looks — ugly! Very, very ugly! This man, as Taverner, was, as you say, near the scene of the murder; as Worthington he got that forged cheque; as Worthington he witnessed Severfield's will! The whole thing —"

"The whole thing's about as black as it can be, Mr. Wendover," interrupted Credding. "And the sooner you and I lay hands on Worthington, *alias* Taverner, Rollinson, the better. Fortunately, I've learnt a bit about him, in addition to what I've told you. He's a member of two sporting clubs — the Persimmon, one; the Craiganour, the other. We can beat him up there, and if we don't find him, we can surely get wind of him. But I've still another man to see on that point — look at that."

He pulled out the wire from the friendly publican, explaining its meaning.

"That'll be about Taverner, *alias* Worthington," he continued. "He's learnt something — he's the sort of chap that's in the know. Let's get a taxi and run along to him."

The friendly publican, in his shirt sleeves and with a large diamond in his cravat, was leaning over the bar in his saloon, in converse with a customer, when Credding and his companions entered his establishment. At sight of him he excused himself from his company and motioned the new-comers to follow him to a private room, the door of which he carefully closed.

"And how are you, my boy?" he asked, turning on Credding, with a cock of his eye in the direction of the others. "Friends o' yours, my boy?"

"Friends!" replied Credding, with something like a wink.

"Just so, my boy — and no doubt of your own persuasion," said the landlord. "All serene, my boy! And as it's a cold night, what do you say to a little refreshment while we talk our business? That's right! And you got my wire, my boy?" he asked, as he produced whisky and glasses from a corner cupboard. "Yes, my boy, of course you would, to be sure! Here's the best of it, gentlemen. Yes, I did that bit of business for you, my boy — on the strict q.t., *of* course!"

"About Taverner?" suggested Credding.

"About Taverner, my boy! And not so much blooming mystery about it, neither, my boy, when it came to it. Judicious inquiry, my boy — a word here and a word there. And you will remember, my boy, that I said to you that a lot o' these fellows used more names than one? Same in this case, my boy! Taverner, my boy, is what the lit'ry folk would call a *nom de plume,* my boy, and what the lawyers call an *alias,* for a man whose rightful name is Worthington. He's a bit of a commission agent, and a bit of a tout, and a bit of anything connected with the gee-gees, my boy. Don't know the man myself: he don't patronise me — that is, of course, as far as I'm aware of: he may ha' been in here, and again he mayn't. But I have ascertained where he does go, my boy — for your sake!"

"That's the ticket!" said Credding. "Where?"

"Well, my boy, for one thing, he's a member of the Persimmon Club, as you thought he might be, and no doubt he could be heard of there. But I know one better than that, my boy — I'm told that he can be found, any night, at Balsamo's."

"Balsamo's?" asked Credding. "Where's that?"

"Balsamo's Restaurant, my boy — one o' these here Italian places in Soho — close by the Royalty Theatre, my boy, is Balsamo's. And this here Worthington, otherwise — or, as I should say, *alias* — Taverner, has a fondness for it, I understand — favours the cooking, my boy, so I'm told — and that, as a general thing, he can be found there any night about eight o'clock, which appears to be his dinner hour."

"Much obliged to you," said Credding. "Very useful information!"

"You're welcome, my boy — you and me being pals," remarked the publican. "Always willing to do a bit for a friend, my boy!"

He was just then called away to another part of his premises, and Wendover and the two detectives, left alone with their newly-acquired information, proceeded to discuss it.

"He may be at this Balsamo's, and he mayn't," remarked Credding. "My belief is that he won't be there! I should say, considering what I saw last night, and that Colinrake's not been at his office nor his flat since, that both Worthington *alias* Taverner, and Colinrake — and the girl — have taken a quiet departure for the Continent! If only we'd been twenty-four hours sooner!"

"Worth trying this restaurant, anyway," remarked Rollinson.

"Oh, we'll try it! "said Credding. "Try anything and anywhere! We'd better get round there now. You'll come along, Mr. Wendover? — there may be something to interest you."

"What do you propose to do?" asked Wendover. "Watch at the door?"

"I want my dinner," replied Credding. "I was in such a hurry to run down to Brighton that I only got a bit of a snack at midday. I propose we go to this Balsamo's and dine — and keep our eyes open."

"You're the only man who can recognise him," remarked Rollinson." You've seen him already."

"In the barber's shop-yes," agreed Credding. "I don't suppose he'd recognise me, though: if he gave a mere glance it would be about all. Well — Balsamo's, then?"

Balsamo's proved to be a typical Italian restaurant, of the sort common in Soho, with a uniformed porter and two shrubs in ornamental plant-pots at the door, a profusion of gilt-framed mirrors inside, and the usual furnishing of red plush seats around the walls. On either side the inner entrance were alcoves, with tables in them; one of these being empty, Credding at once made for it, motioning his companions to follow him.

"Good spot this," he muttered as they sat down. "We can see right along the room from here — what's more, we can notice everybody who comes in without being noticed ourselves. And to begin with we order our dinners. And take no notice of anybody. Or pretend not to! Leave it to me to spot him — if he's here, or if he should come."

Wendover fell in with the detective's suggestion, but when he had given his order to the waiter and passed the menu over to his companions he took an apparently casual and careless glance at his surroundings. The restaurant was a place of one not very capacious room, long rather than wide, with tables running down either side of it, a service bar at one further corner, a counter for wines at another. It was fairly full and the company was of the sort that can be found in any restaurant in that quarter of London at any time, with the artistic and theatrical element strongly pre-dominating. But amongst the dozen or so of the men there, Wendover saw none that corresponded to Credding's description of the man they wanted.

"Not here, Mr. Wendover," murmured Credding suddenly. "I've seen the lot, without seeming to see. However, we'll live in hopes. It's scarcely eight o'clock, and —"

At that moment the inner door close by them swung open and a man, tall, heavy, strode in and, looking neither to right nor left, marched swiftly up the floor towards the far end of the room, nodding familiarly to the waiters as he passed them. One waiter evidently expected this man and had kept a place for him; as the new-comer dropped into it this waiter produced the materials for an *aperitif* and set them before him. And Credding whispered to his fellow-watchers:

"There he is!" he said. "The luck's running good to-day! That's the man! Now, all we've got to do is to let him get his dinner while we get ours: then it'll be time to start operations. Here! — I'll come round that side of the table, so that I shall have my back to him. You can keep an eye on him, Rollinson, and when he starts to leave, we leave too."

Worthington was in no haste to leave. He appeared to be of leisurely habits. He was leisurely over his dinner and leisurely over the cigar and coffee that succeeded it. It was past nine o'clock when he strode away from his seat, again paying no attention to any other customers, and walked out into the entrance. He started when Credding, with Rollinson in close attendance, tapped him on the shoulder — but the detectives, keenly observant, saw that the start was one of ordinary surprise; evidently the man was in no expectation of being stopped.

"A word with you, sir," said Credding. "Mr. Worthington, I believe?"

Worthington looked from one man to the other, then at Wendover in the background.

"What d'ye want?" he demanded brusquely. "Strangers to me!"

"You're not a stranger to me, Mr. Worthington," answered Credding. "I've had you under observation since yesterday evening, right from the time you left your rooms at 37, Thamesdale Avenue, Richmond. The fact is, we're police officers, and we must ask you to go to Scotland Yard with us — we want to put a few questions to you."

Worthington's big jaw had dropped, and a black expression had stolen over his face.

"What about?" he asked sharply.

"A good many things," replied Credding. "You'll hear when we get there. Take my advice, and come along, Mr. Worthington. We can get a cab close by here."

Worthington stood for a minute, silent, staring.

"Is it that Severfield affair?" he asked suddenly. "Because if it is, the man you want —"

"The man we want just now, Mr. Worthington, is you!" interrupted Credding. "If you've any information to give, come along, where you can give it in privacy!"

Chapter XXIII
Under Examination

Half an hour later Wendover, seated in the background of a small, sombre room, found himself deeply and curiously interested in watching and listening to the preliminary fencing between Worthington and the police officials. Worthington, obviously, wanted to know what the police knew; the police, and Credding in particular, wanted to draw Worthington out. For a while both resembled wrestlers finessing for a grip: Worthington's patience gave out first.

"Look you here!" he suddenly burst out. "I know a good deal about this Severfield affair — murder, you call it, no doubt, and murder it may have been for all I know! But if you think I'm mixed up in it, or in anything that's to do with it, in a fashion that would bring me within your power, within the law, you're making a bloomer! — and that's a fact!"

"In that case, Mr. Worthington, there's no reason why you shouldn't tell us all you know," remarked Credding. "I suggest you should tell us! Why not?"

"On the usual understanding," said an official who had been brought in. "That anything he says may be used as evid —"

"Oh, rot to that!" exclaimed Worthington. "You can't bring any charge against me so the evidence business won't come in, see? Anyhow, if you do bring any charge against me, you'll be wrong. As I say, I know a good deal — but there's nothing in it that can incriminate me. I've clean hands — if another hasn't."

"We shall be glad to hear about the other who hasn't," remarked Credding.

Worthington said nothing more for a moment. He looked carefully at the men facing him, and at Wendover sitting on one side.

"Which of you lot was it that called on my banker at Richmond the other day, and at my rooms there?" he demanded suddenly.

"I called," replied Credding. "And that gentleman called with me — Mr. Wendover, solicitor to Messrs. Bridgwater, the bankers. Mr. Bridgwater was with us."

"And what might you want to know, pray?" asked Worthington.

"We wanted to know about a cheque for fifty thousand pounds drawn in your favour by the late Mr. Severfield," replied the detective.

"What about the cheque?"

"That cheque, Mr. Worthington, has been pronounced a forgery! There's no doubt it is a forgery. We wanted to know what you know about it — we want to know now."

Worthington let out an exclamation of contemptuous disdain.

"Forgery be damned!" he said. "Who says it's a forgery?"

"We'll not go into that," answered Credding. "It is declared to have been forged. Take it at that. If you can tell anything about it — how and why you got it —"

Worthington began to look puzzled. He stared at Credding as if ideas were coming into his mind that were surprisingly new.

"Look here!" he said. "If I'm going to talk, you'll talk first. I'm sure of my position, d'ye see? What do you know about me? You said you tracked me last night. Why?"

"I know a good deal," replied Credding. "You use the name of Taverner —"

"Taverner is my name," interrupted Worthington. "John Taverner Xavier Worthington!"

"Very well — we know that," said Credding. "Under the name of Taverner you stopped at the Beaumanor Hotel at Brighton last August —"

"Openly — openly," muttered Worthington.

"Quite openly! Under the same name, you took Elvescot, a bungalow near Black Rock, for six months, from Mrs. Rathbourne."

"Well — anything wrong about that?"

"Nothing! But on the night of October 15th — the night on which Severfield was murdered close by there — you were in the neighbourhood, in a car, in company with another man."

"Well? — and is there anything wrong about that?"

"That's as may be! You went to Welford, at his garage, at the corner turning down to Black Rock, and bought a second-hand spanner from him."

"Well — and what if I did? I did!"

"That spanner was found near Severfield's body! We've no doubt that it was with that spanner that Severfield was struck down."

Worthington nodded his head two or three times, slowly.

"I've wondered, more than once, where that spanner got to," he remarked. "I missed it — next day. Concluded I'd dropped it on the roadside. Well, well! — and you think Severfield was struck with it?"

"We do!" affirmed Credding.

"And may be," continued Worthington, with a sneer, "you think I struck him? Now then, let me put something to you, and let's see how it strikes your intelligent minds! I've said I called at Welford's garage. I've said I got an old spanner there. Now do you think that if I'd had any intention of harming Severfield at that bungalow, or anywhere near, on that night, I should have openly called at a garage close by where, mind you, my face and appearance was well known, or at any rate ought to ha' been, considering I'd lived near it for a month, only a short time before; do you think that's likely? Rot!"

"That's one to you, certainly," said Credding. "So — what were you doing there?"

Worthington became silent again for a while, watching the expectant faces. He suddenly fastened on Credding once more.

"What did you see of me last night?" he demanded. "You followed me!"

"Followed you from the hairdresser at the corner of Thamesdale Avenue to Number 37," replied Credding. "From there to your bank manager's residence, next to the bank. Thence to certain flats in Shaftesbury Avenue. You came out in Colinrake's company. The two of you went to Madresfield Mansions, where Miss Beatrix Greville lives. You came out of there and went to the Amaryllis Club and got Miss Greville. And you drove off with her. That sufficient?"

"Have you got Colinrake?" asked Worthington sharply.

"Not yet!" replied the detective.

"Colinrake is the man you should get, then! I know certain things — but he knows... pretty well all, I should say." He paused again for a moment. "That cheque?" he exclaimed. "Who's pronounced it a forgery?"

"The leading expert of the day!" answered Credding. "Undoubted!"

"If it is a forgery," said Worthington slowly, "I know nothing about it — and I've been done! Colinrake..." He became silent once more, evidently thinking. "I've no objection to tell all I know!" he added suddenly. "There's something wrong, and it'll be best to have it out."

"Far best!" agreed Credding.

"Well, I'll tell you!" continued Worthington. "If I'd had any idea about that cheque, I'd have been to you before. It's this way — I've known Colinrake for some years — done a little betting with him, and met him at clubs and at race meetings and so on: you might say we were pretty close acquaintances. I've been at his office: I've met Severfield there and done a bit of business with him. Now then, which will you have first? — the cheque business or the bungalow visit?"

"The bungalow," replied Credding.

"Well, that's easy told!" said Worthington. "Monday, October 16th, you say was the date. That's right — Monday, and that Monday it was. Well, on the night before, Colinrake came to me at the Persimmon Club, latish on, and told me that Severfield wanted to take a quiet little place at Brighton for a month or six weeks. Colinrake knew I had Elvescot on my hands until February, and that my wife and I —"

"Just a minute, if you please," interrupted Credding. "The mention of your wife reminds me of a question I want to put to you. Where do you live — your regular residence?"

"High Barnet," responded Worthington promptly. "Number 3, Middlesex Villas."

"Then — this place at Richmond?"

"Temporary lodgings — where I go for a day or two at a time. I've a lot of business Richmond way. But I live — where I've said."

"Well — you were saying," suggested Credding.

"Saying that Colinrake knew I'd Elvescot on my hands till February and that my wife and I didn't think of going down there again," continued Worthington. "He wanted to know if I'd power to sub-let the place. I said I certainly understood that I had that power — to a satisfactory and respectable tenant. He then said that it was just the place to suit Severfield, and that he'd get him to run down to Brighton and look at it. He asked me to call at his office in Southampton Street next day. I called. Colinrake then told me that Severfield was going to Brighton that afternoon and that we were to meet him at Elvescot in the evening, from, say, eight-thirty to nine.? He suggested that he and I should go down by the five-thirty-five from Victoria, dine when we got there, and go on to the gimgalow. I said no, I could beat that — I had my car in town, and as it was a fine day we'd go in that, and dine at the Chequers, at Horley. Colinrake agreed. We left London at five o'clock, got to Horley, and we did dine at the Chequers, where I'm well known. No secrecy about it, mind you! — all that I did was done openly, all through."

"Well?" said Credding.

"When we left Horley, we went on to Brighton, usual way, and through the town to the Newhaven road. When we got to near where Welford's garage is, something went wrong with the car — it had been a bit queer all the way. As we had the prospect of going home in it, I went across to Welford's for a spanner — I hadn't one in my repairing outfit. I knew Welford's place by sight, and him, too, though I'd never been there before, because when me and my wife were at Elvescot, we hadn't a car — I bought mine soon after leaving there — but I'd seen Welford at his door, in passing, when we were about there, and I thought he recognised me. I got a spanner from him, and went back to the car with it. Now, then, you say that spanner was found near Severfield's body?"

"Close by!" replied Credding.

"How do you know it was the same spanner? All spanners are pretty much of a muchness!"

"Welford identified it as the one he sold to you."

"He may have been mistaken, though. But suppose it was? — the fact is, that after going back to my car with it, I never saw it again!"

"How was that?" asked Credding.

Worthington held up both hands.

"I've weak wrists," he answered. "No power in them! Always been like that. And I couldn't do what was necessary with that spanner. I was for going to the garage and fetching a mechanic, but Colinrake said he'd try. I handed the spanner to him. I never saw it again — I don't know what became of it. I remembered it, next day, when the car was being cleaned up at home, but I couldn't find it. I thought Colinrake had probably dropped it or laid it down on the roadside — and he may have done, for all I know, or you know, either."

"And he may have slipped it into his overcoat pocket!" muttered Credding. "But go on!"

"Well, we went up the road to the bungalow, of which, of course, I'd a key. I put the car in a narrow lane, a bit farther along the road on the opposite side, and turned the lights off — I knew it would be safe there, as the lane only leads into some fields. I let Colinrake and myself into Elvescot — I'd taken a lamp with me. It would be about nine o'clock, I think, then. Colinrake said he'd given Severfield full instructions as to the whereabouts of the place, and we expected him any minute: we thought he'd drive up in a cab. He didn't come. And as a matter of fact, Severfield never did come!"

"Never came to Elvescot at all?" exclaimed Credding.

"Never! I never saw a sign of him!" answered Worthington. "After we'd been there a bit, Colinrake said he'd go outside and see if he could see or hear anything of him. He did so, and he was away about half an hour, perhaps a bit more, leaving me by myself in the bungalow. He came back at last — alone. He said Severfield evidently wasn't coming, and we might as well go home. I suggested going back to Brighton and calling at Severfield's hotel: Colinrake said he didn't know which hotel he was at, and it wasn't worth while. So we set off, and at Colinrake's suggestion we went round by Newhaven and Lewes —"

"And stopped outside the Castle Hotel at Newhaven for a while, I believe?" interrupted Credding.

"To put some water in the car — yes," admitted Worthington. "Yes — that's right. After that, round by Lewes and across country into the usual road and home. I set Colinrake down at Piccadilly Circus and went home to High Barnet."

"When did you hear of Severfield's death?" asked Credding.

"Latish in the afternoon of the following day."

"Where were you at the time?"

"Persimmon Club. I saw it in an evening paper."

"What did you do?"

"Made for Colinrake's office, of course. He wasn't in — he'd gone to Brighton. I called later — kept going back until I found him there. He'd just got in when I did find him."

"And what did he say?"

"He said that we knew now why Severfield had never turned up at Elvescot. He'd got on the path by the cliff at the foot of the field below the garden, and had fallen over and broken his neck."

"You believed that?"

"I believed it then, and I don't know that I was wrong, either! You don't know how that mark on his forehead was caused! — it's all surmise as to what caused it, I reckon!"

"Leave that!" said Credding. "Now, knowing what you did — why didn't you come forward?"

Chapter XXIV
The Telephone Rings

For the first time since this informal examination had begun, Worthington showed some signs of embarrassment. He hesitated to reply, and he shook his head as if in doubt of some past proceeding.

"I'll admit that I ought to have come forward," he answered at last. "I wish I had! — now. But I was influenced by Colinrake. Of course he's a solicitor. What's more, he was Severfield's solicitor. I knew him to be hand-in-glove with Severfield."

"Did you know that of your own knowledge?" asked the high official who had presided over these proceedings, more or less silently, but very watchfully. "Is that your opinion, from what you'd seen of the two men?"

"Well, not so much from what I'd seen as from what Colinrake had told me," replied Worthington. "He was always telling me of his influence with Severfield, and how Severfield was more and more leaving things in his hands — his affairs, you know."

"Money affairs?"

"Yes, money affairs. I knew for a fact that they had considerable dealings — big dealings — in that way. Of course, I have seen them together — met them together — I've had lunch with Severfield in company with Colinrake, in Severfield's rooms at his hotel. I knew that Severfield employed Colinrake a good deal — made a confidential servant of him, in point of fact."

"Well, what did Colinrake say about the news from Brighton — about what you were both to do?"

"He said — to say nothing. There was no doubt, he said, that Severfield, seeking the bungalow, had got on that path by the edge of the cliff and had fallen over and broken his neck, and the coroner's jury would be sure to bring in a verdict of death by misadventure. There was no need for us to say anything at all. Nobody but ourselves knew that we'd had an appointment with Severfield that night, and it was not at all likely that anybody would ever find out that we'd been at Elvescot. If that was found out, he said, we'd a perfectly good explanation to give, but he didn't see how it could be found out. The best thing, in view of everything, was to hold our tongues."

"What did he mean by 'in view of everything'?" asked Credding.

"Well, I suppose he meant — I should say, now, he meant — in view of the fact that he and I had been in the neighbourhood! That might have been thought — suspicious."

"But neither of you were to benefit by Severfield's death," remarked the high official, "were you?"

"I wasn't anyway! I don't know about Colinrake. He didn't tell me that he was. But that's what he advised — to keep our tongues still. He was dead certain it had been an accident and that the jury would return a verdict to that effect at the end of the coroner's inquest — all we'd got to do was to lie low, and the thing would right itself."

"Very well!" said Credding. "You took his advice and said nothing to anybody?"

"Never mentioned it to a soul, of course. I thought Colinrake — being a lawyer — knew what was best."

"Well," continued Credding, "what about this cheque for fifty thousand pounds, drawn in your favour by Severfield, which the leading expert of the day declares is a forgery?"

"It's news to me! I don't know that it's a forgery. If it's a forgery, why did they honour it all right at Bridgwater's bank? They never questioned it in any way — according to my bankers."

"Never mind that! How came you in possession of it?"

"That requires a bit of telling," replied Worthington. "It came to me in the course of a transaction — a perfectly straightforward transaction, as far as I'm concerned! And I'll just tell you this! — if you can find any transaction of mine that hasn't been straightforward, you're welcome! But — however you try — you can't!"

"Never mind that, either," said Credding. "Tell us about this cheque."

"The cheque came to me from Severfield through Colinrake," said Worthington. "Colinrake told me — it would be about a fortnight or so before Severfield died — that Severfield would like to own and run, and of course, train, two or three really good race-horses, and that he was willing to put money in my hands to buy him some likely and promising youngsters. Colinrake asked — on Severfield's behalf — what sum I'd like, to be laid out in that way. After thinking it over, and finding that he didn't want to go beyond a string of five or six, I suggested that he should let me have £ 30,000 to lay out. A few days after that — I should say within a week of Severfield's death — Colinrake handed me that cheque for £ 50,000. It was made out to me. Colinrake said that he'd been with Severfield that morning, and Severfield had given him some instructions for the investment of £ 20,000, so had made out a cheque to include both amounts. I took the £ 50,000 cheque and there and then gave Colinrake a cheque of my own for £ 20,000 — the difference. I paid Severfield's cheque into my bank that day, and it was duly honoured at Bridgwater's."

"And I suppose the cheque you gave Colinrake — for £ 20,000 — was duly honoured at your bank?"

"Of course it was!"

"At once?"

"It would be honoured, naturally, the moment it was presented! You can see my passbook with pleasure! All this'll be entered up there. What you mean about Severfield's cheque being forged, I don't know! Who forged it? I saw nothing wrong about it — though, to be sure, I did no more than give a mere glance at it. I know Severfield's writing, well enough!"

"Did you ever see Severfield, personally, about this buying of horses?"

"No!"

"Did you ever see him at all, after getting that cheque?"

"No, I never did! The whole transaction was done through Colinrake."

"Well — have you bought any horses with the £ 30,000?"

"Not yet. Of course, Severfield's death put a stop to that."

"Then the money — where is the money? The £ 30,000?"

"In my bank, of course!"

"Untouched?"

"Of course it's untouched! If you want to know, it's part of my balance — a pretty considerable one. I'm not a man of straw, mind you!"

"Glad to hear it!" remarked Credding. "Well, now, you went over to Paris almost immediately after Severfield's death, didn't you?"

"I did! — the day after I heard of it."

"Why?"

"Business! I've a partnership in a business in Paris — I often go across. And there's nothing underhand or secret about that, either. The business is an old-established one, and you're welcome to whatever information you want about it."

"Well, you're very ready to give information, Mr. Worthington," said Credding, "so perhaps you'll say why you and Colinrake went after the young lady. Miss Greville, to the Amaryllis Club last night? What was your reason?"

"That was Colinrake's notion. When I found that you'd been inquiring for me at my bank and at my Richmond address, I suspected that you were police, and that your call had something to do with the Severfield affair: I thought you'd probably got wind of the presence of Colinrake and myself at Elvescot on the night of Severfield's death. So I went off to Colinrake. I'd got a description of you from my bank manager, and I gave it to Colinrake. He said at once that he knew who you were, and he became anxious to know if you'd been to Miss Greville. We went to her flat — then to that dancing club. Colinrake insisted on her coming away with him, there and then — I went with them. But only a little way. I got out of their cab at the corner of Oxford Circus, and went home."

"Which home?" asked Credding.

"My home at High Barnet. The Richmond place is, as I've told you, an occasional temporary lodging."

"And you haven't seen either Colinrake or Miss Greville since you left them last night at Oxford Circus?"

"I haven't! Neither of 'em."

"Where were they going when you left them?"

"To her flat, as far as I know. But I don't know — they might have been going to his."

"Did Colinrake question Miss Greville about any visits?"

"Yes! She'd had none. That is, she'd had none from you and your like."

"Did Colinrake seem alarmed by what you told him?"

"He did not! Curious, perhaps — but not alarmed. He mentioned you, and said you and Mr. Wendover and Mr. Bridgwater had all got bees in your bonnets and were running your heads against a wall. No! — he didn't show alarm."

Credding turned to Wendover with a smile. And Wendover, leaning forward, whispered two words.

"The will?"

"Better inquire into that yourself, Mr. Wendover," Credding whispered back. "You'll know better than I shall about what questions to put. Mr. Worthington," he continued, turning to the unwilling yet accommodating visitor, "you've answered all we've asked very readily, and now Mr. Wendover here, as solicitor for Messrs. Bridgwaters, the bankers with whom Severfield dealt, wants some information from you on another matter. That's Severfield's will."

Worthington looked questioningly at Wendover. There was a faint suspicion in his look which Wendover was quick to notice.

"What about Severfield's will?" he asked. "You aren't going to tell me that there's something wrong about that, too? — like the cheque?"

"Suppose he did?" asked Credding, before Wendover could reply. "What then? What's in your mind?"

Worthington threw out his hands with an expressive gesture.

"I've been thinking, or beginning to think, as you've gone on, and especially about that cheque, that I've been done!" he exclaimed, with some show of indignation. "And hang me! if I ever thought I was an easy man for anybody to do! — don't ever remember anybody doing me before! But — it looks like it! And... by Colinrake! For look you here," he went on, his manner becoming truculent and vehement, "if that damned cheque is a forgery, who could ha' forged it but Colinrake? From Colinrake it came! — not from Severfield. And now I hear all this about it, that £ 20,000 that Colinrake had out of it comes up pretty prominent, don't it? Colinrake —"

"Just let me ask you a few questions about Severfield's will," interrupted Wendover quietly. "We shall know more — and so will you — if you answer them. We have seen the will, and your name appears on it as one of the two attesting witnesses, Colinrake being the other. You did sign it?"

"Oh, I signed, right enough!" agreed Worthington. "That's so!"

"Where were you when you signed?"

"Colinrake's office."

"You had, of course, seen Severfield sign it first — in your presence, and in Colinrake's — the two of you being present together when Severfield signed?"

"Severfield nothing!" exclaimed Worthington. "Severfield wasn't there!"

Wendover with difficulty repressed an exclamation of surprise; the high official, sitting by and listening keenly, sniffed audibly and then smiled; he and Wendover exchanged glances.

"Severfield was not there when you signed his will as witness?" said Wendover. "Is that definite? You didn't sign it in his presence?"

"Of course I didn't!" answered Worthington testily. "When I signed the thing, Severfield was dead!"

A curious silence fell on the room. Of the six or seven men assembled in it, Worthington, the centre of interest, appeared to be the only one who failed to understand the significance of what he had just admitted. The detectives looked at each other and smiled, covertly; Wendover and the presiding official exchanged another meaning glance. And the silence was broken by Worthington.

"What is all this about that will, anyway?" he asked. "I'm no lawyer! — don't understand anything about wills — never signed one in my life before. Colinrake said it would be all right —"

"Just tell us how you came to sign it — and exactly when," interrupted Wendover. "Tell us the precise details."

"No details about it!" answered Worthington. "Seemed quite an ordinary matter at the time — to me, at any rate. It was when I went into Colinrake's office to find out if he'd heard about Severfield's death, and found him just come back from Brighton. He mentioned that Severfield's will was in his hands but it wasn't completed; it wanted, he said, another signature by somebody who knew Severfield's writing. 'Here,' he said, 'you know Severfield's signature well enough; just shove yours there, beneath mine.' Well, I tell you, I'm no lawyer — I don't know anything about wills — I haven't made my own yet — and of course I took Colinrake at his word. I saw Severfield's signature, plain enough, and knew it for his, so I signed at the place Colinrake pointed out, and he said that was all right and locked the will up in a safe. That's all I know about it."

"Did he tell you the contents of the will?" asked Wendover.

"He did not! Never said a word about them."

"Then you don't know what the provisions of the will were?"

"No, I don't! I know nothing whatever about Severfield's will except what I've told you — that I signed it under Colinrake's orders." Wendover nodded to the high official as a sign that he had no more to ask Worthington, and Worthington, interpreting the nod rightly, made a gesture of impatience.

"Gentlemen! I want to go home!" he said. "I've told you all I know! If you want more out of me, I'm willing to come here to-morrow morning. But now I want to get home to my house — I want to see my wife! Can I go now?"

Before replying to this direct question, the high official and the detectives drew together and talked for a while in whispers. Finally the high official turned to Worthington.

"You may go!" he said. "But — just to verify your statement about your house at High Barnet — one of my men will go with you. And I shall want to see you again, to-morrow morning, at ten o'clock — here. Rollinson, you go with him."

"I've got my car in Long Acre," said Worthington. "If he'll come up there with me, I'll drive him along to my house and give him a good glass of whisky when we get there, and he can easily get back. Ten o'clock tomorrow, here? Depend on me!"

When Rollinson and Worthington had gone, Wendover and Credding went too. Orridge, said Wendover, had promised to ring him up at his flat if he ever wanted him after office hours; Credding had better come there, for the night. It was well after ten when they got there: for an hour they sat discussing Worthington's disclosures. At midnight nothing had happened — but ten minutes after twelve the telephone bell rang.

Chapter XXV
The Telephone Rings Again

Wendover hurried out to the hall of his flat with Credding, eager and impatient, at his heels. Both expected the summons to come from Orridge — but the voice carried to Wendover was an unfamiliar one.

"That Mr. Wendover? Right! — this is Scotland Yard. Is Credding with you?"

"Here!" replied Wendover. "At my elbow."

"Tell him Rollinson has just telephoned from Worthington's house at High Barnet. He says that on reaching there Mrs. Worthington told them that Colinrake called, asking for Worthington, at half-past eleven, just before they arrived. Colinrake said he must see Worthington and would call again during the night. We suggest Credding should get up there at once."

"We shall both go — just now," answered Wendover. He rang off after another word or two and, after repeating the message to Credding, began to hustle into an overcoat.

"We can get a cab at the corner, Credding," he said. "Always one or two in readiness throughout the night there. High Barnet? — that's about ten miles from where we are. As it's midnight, we'll do it in half an hour. Colinrake there! — what's that mean?"

"That things are coming to a crisis, Mr. Wendover!" replied Credding grimly. "That's about it! And I only hope we catch him when we get to Worthington's! — it'll save a lot of trouble!"

Three-quarters of an hour later, Worthington himself opened the door of his house to them and shook his head before Credding could get out an inquiry.

"Not been back!" he said. "But from what he said to my wife, he'll certainly come! You'd better hear what she says."

"Wait a minute!" replied Credding. He stepped back from the door and took a careful look at his surroundings, seen dimly in the lights from the windows and in the faint glow of the autumn moon. Worthington's house was a detached one — of the sort known to auctioneers and the property market as highly desirable villa residences. It stood in a large garden, thickly bordered with shrubs and fenced in by a ring of trees: the front door of the house was approached by a gravelled carriage drive, on which now stood the taxicab in which Wendover and Credding had hurried from Sloane Square. This carriage drive, passing the door and the front of the house, terminated amongst the shrubs before a tiled shed, obviously used as a garage.

Credding beckoned Worthington down the steps from the door.

"What did you and Rollinson do as soon as you drove up here?" he asked. "You'd bring your car in here, of course?"

"Of course — usual thing," assented Worthington. "Do? Why, nothing! Except to put my car in the shed yonder."

"Rollinson help you at that?" inquired Credding.

"Gave a hand — just to shove her in," said Worthington. "Why?"

"Talking while you were at that?" continued the detective.

"We were talking — yes!"

"About the doings of the night, I suppose?" suggested Credding.

"To be sure — been talking about them all the way up."

"And no doubt mentioned Colinrake's name while you were at that shed?" said Credding. "His name would come up, eh?"

"I dare say! We were talking about him. But what —"

"Just this! — that there's not much likelihood of Colinrake coming back again!" said Credding. "You may be perfectly sure that Colinrake was hanging about when you came home! Probably in the garden, amongst these bushes. And when he saw you with a strange man, and heard his own name mentioned — why, it's obvious what he'd do. Clear out! He'll not come back. However —"

"Well, I never saw any sign of him," said Worthington. "I'll tell you what I did see, though. There was a taxicab waiting a bit down the road — a hundred yards away or so. drawn up under the trees."

"That would be his," said Credding. "Of course, he watched for you! And he may know Rollinson by sight, as a C.I.D. man. He'll not come back — he's off! Still — let's hear what Mrs. Worthington says."

196

Wendover had come up during this conversation: Rollinson followed him, in time to overhear Worthington's remark about the taxicab at the roadside.

"I was a bit suspicious about that cab," he remarked. "Struck me as odd that a taxi should be waiting there at that time."

"Pity you didn't invent an excuse to question the driver, then!" remarked Credding. "You might have had Colinrake safe by this time! Well — let's hear about him."

Worthington led them into his house and introduced Mrs. Worthington. Credding saw at once that she answered the description given him by the caretaker of Elvescot and the landlord of the Beaumanor Hotel of Mrs. Taverner. She was evidently a woman not easily upset or put out, and she gave her account of Colinrake's visit calmly and circumstantially.

"He came to the front door there just about ten minutes before Mr. Worthington and this gentleman arrived," she said. "Of course, I know Mr. Colinrake well enough; he's been here many a time. This time he seemed in a hurry — agitated-like — never said 'how d'ye do?' nor nothing, but asked, sharp, if Worthington was at home? I said no, he wasn't, and I didn't know that he would be home, though he might — I thought it was very likely he would. Then I asked him if he wouldn't come in. He said he wouldn't — just then, at any rate; there was somebody else he wanted to see, he said; he'd come back, and in any case, he'd be certain to call during the night — he must see Worthington, he said, before morning. He told me to ask Worthington to sit up for him. But — he's not been back since then."

"He'll not come!" muttered Credding aside, to Wendover. "He's spotted Rollinson! That's about it — he must have recognised him while Rollinson and Worthington were putting the car away. Do you know," he went on, turning to Worthington, "if Colinrake knows anybody around here?"

"Not to my knowledge," replied Worthington. "I've never heard him mention anybody. He may do, of course."

Credding turned to Mrs. Worthington.

"Did he mention the name of anybody he wanted to see, ma'am?" he asked.

"He didn't," replied Mrs. Worthington. "He just said there was somebody. Then he hurried off."

Credding drew Wendover aside.

"I don't see any use in stopping here," he murmured. "There's always the chance that your man Orridge may ring you up, any time. You think he's on Colinrake's track?"

"I feel sure he's on Colinrake's track!" affirmed Wendover. "His silence during the last few days is a sure proof — he's waiting till he can report something definite. And for anything we know he may have tracked Colinrake up here — and followed him again when he went away."

"Well — I say, let's get away," said Credding. "I haven't the least belief in Colinrake's coming back after what I've learnt." He motioned Rollinson to follow them out of the room. "Of course, you'll stay here, with Worthington, and bring him down to head-quarters in the morning?" he suggested. "The only thing is the extreme off-chance of Colinrake's return? Personally, I'm sure he won't! — your being here has put him off. But — if he should?"

Rollinson showed some signs of uneasiness.

"Not much chance for me if he turned ugly — and had a gun on him!" he muttered. "Besides," he added, with a glance at the door of the room they had just left, "there'd be two of 'em!"

"I don't think there's any fear of him!" remarked Credding, nodding towards the door behind which Worthington and his wife remained. "Strikes me, he's about fed up with Colinrake — sees he's been done by him! But wait a minute — we'll soon make sure about that!"

He went back to the dining-room and called Worthington out into the hall.

"We don't want to alarm your wife, nor bother her needlessly," he whispered, motioning him to join the other two. "Now look here! — if Colinrake should come back, you're not going to side with him?"

"Not after what I've heard to-night from you fellows!" exclaimed Worthington. "No fear, my boy!"

"If he gave any trouble, you'd help Rollinson here?" suggested Credding.

"And with pleasure!" said Worthington heartily. "Seems to me he's been having me for the mug, pretty considerably! But if what you surmise is right — that he was watching in my garden when we came in — he'll not come back! I don't expect him back. If he should — well, we'll take care of him!"

Credding and Wendover went away, and entering the waiting taxicab, drove back to London. Credding was silent for a while, but when they were speeding down the Finchley Road he suddenly turned to his companion.

"Mr. Wendover!" he said, "I've come to a conclusion about this Severfield affair! And to start with, I believe this man Worthington has told us the truth."

"Worthington," replied Wendover," strikes me as the sort of man who might be sharp enough in his own business, but extremely simple outside it. If he told us the truth he's unusually gullible!"

"Well, I don't know that he is, Mr. Wendover," said Credding. "I don't see that one needs to be very gullible to be taken in by such an affair as that cheque transaction, for instance. I think Worthington took that cheque in all good faith, believing Colinrake's account about it. Colinrake is a plausible fellow — his story was well invented, because, when you come to think of it, what was there that was unusual in a very wealthy man like Severfield wanting to buy and own a few good race-horses? Nothing! I honestly believe Worthington in that matter."

"He was gullible about the will," said Wendover.

"And I don't know about that!" replied Credding. "We're not all lawyers, you know. I dare say there are plenty of folk who don't know the law's requirements about witnessing a will — I'm sure there was a time when I didn't! And you see, all through, Worthington has evidently been under Colinrake's influence — what Colinrake told him, he believed. No! — I think we've got a fine witness in Worthington!"

"If Worthington is telling the absolute truth about the visit to the bungalow on the night of Severfield's murder — yes!" said Wendover. "The question is — is he? For don't you overlook the strength of the case against him, Credding! Look how it can be put! He's one of two men involved in the production of a will which is probably forged, but is certainly irregular and will almost positively be pronounced invalid; he is mixed up with the handling of a forged cheque for a heavy amount. Will and cheque together, there was a strong motive for the removal of Severfield on the part of these two men, and if one looks at the facts apart from Worthington's presentation of them, one can easily believe that when they went to Elvescot that night they meant to get rid of Severfield — both of them!"

"No doubt! — but, you see, I believe in Worthington's presentation of the facts," replied Credding. "Worthington raised a strong point when he asked if it was likely if he was going to murder, or assist in murdering Severfield at that bungalow, that he would call at that garage close by and carry off that spanner! That's not likely! — it's a strong point, I say. No — my belief is that when Colinrake went out to meet Severfield, Colinrake had that spanner in his coat pocket. He met Severfield, lured him down to the cliff, stunned him, and threw the body over the edge — that's about it!"

"If that is really what happened, nobody but Colinrake himself can tell the exact truth," remarked Wendover. "What rather puzzles me is that when Worthington heard the news about Severfield, he didn't suspect Colinrake. He knew Colinrake had been out of the bungalow looking about for Severfield for some time — why, when he heard what had taken place, didn't he put two and two together, and get a suspicion?"

"Because, there again, he believed in Colinrake," said Credding, "and what's more, you must remember that at that time, as far as we're aware, he'd no reason to doubt him. No! — I want to see Worthington in the witness-box — and Colinrake in the dock! And I wish we could hear of Colinrake!"

But there was no message from Orridge awaiting them when they reached Wendover's flat, and nothing came to disturb the few hours' sleep which they got before the late dawn broke. Credding slept badly — he was chasing people up and down; careering round in swiftly-driven cars; inextricably muddled in a whirl of rapid progress up this street, down the next, and round innumerable corners. And in the midst of it there came a ceaseless ringing in his ears — and at last, just as the grey light was becoming evident in his room, he realised that somebody was ringing up Wendover on the telephone outside his door.

Credding had the gift of becoming wide-awake on the instant, and within a second of opening, his eyes he was out of bed and answering the call. And as he had expected, it was Orridge's voice that he heard.

"Mr. Wendover?"

"No — Credding!" replied the detective. "At Mr. Wendover's flat. What is it?"

"This is Orridge speaking. Look here, Credding, can you get help and come down here quick — City?"

"Yes — where?"

"Meet me Metropolitan Railway Station, Aldgate: I'll be on the look-out. Be careful! Colinrake's at the Three Nuns Hotel, close by."

"Certain of that?" asked Credding.

"Of course! Tracked him there last night. Get some help and come along — I've an idea he's leaving early. The girl's there, too."

"Right!" answered Credding. He turned to Wendover, who had come hurrying into the hall, and hastily told him Orridge's news. "We'll get a couple of men from the Yard and get down there as fast as we can," he added. "What's the time? — nearly eight o'clock. Better hurry, Mr. Wendover!"

"If Orridge has his eye on Colinrake, he won't lose sight of him," remarked Wendover presently, as they set out for the nearest cab rank. "But if he tracked him to this hotel last night, Orridge must have been up at High Barnet. If that's so —"

"Oh, I'm through with speculations, Mr. Wendover!" exclaimed Credding. "I want to get to solid fact now — which means to lay hands on Colinrake —"

"You'll arrest him?" said Wendover.

"You'll see about that, sir, when I get near enough!" answered the detective. "My only anxiety now is lest Colinrake should have gone before we're down there. Orridge, for all we know, is single-handed, and Colinrake's wily enough to take no chances, in my opinion."

Orridge, waiting outside the rendezvous when Wendover, Credding, and the two detectives they had secured at Scotland Yard drove up. looked confident enough, and his answer to Credding's sharp question was decided.

"They're in the hotel all right," he answered. "I'll tell you everything afterwards, but I tracked 'em there last night — they came here about ten and retired. I took a room here myself, to keep in touch. They marked the call-board to be called at nine o'clock this morning. It's a quarter to nine now. You've got Colinrake safe, right enough!"

"We'll make sure at once, anyway!" said Credding. He looked his two detective companions over, and nodded at one. "Here!" he said. "You come with me into the hotel — the rest of you come up to the front, cautiously Now, Orridge, what name are these two under — not their own, of course?"

"Mr. and Mrs. Campbell," answered Orridge. "Room 55."

Credding went swiftly to the main entrance of the hotel, and after a glance round, approached a uniformed hall-porter.

"I want to see Mr. Campbell," he said. "Staying in Room 55. Do you know if he's down yet?"

An under-porter, busied with some luggage close by, turned quickly.

"Mr. and Mrs. Campbell have gone, sir!" he exclaimed. "They went half an hour ago!"

Chapter XXVI
The Wire to Liverpool

Credding let out a smothered imprecation and turned half savagely on the man who had spoken.

"Gone!" he exclaimed. "You're sure?"

"Saw 'em go — myself!" replied the man. He pointed to an entrance opposite to that by which the detective and his companions had come in. "They went that way," he added. "Side street!"

"On foot?" demanded Credding. He was fuming with impatience and could scarcely keep still to ask questions. "Tell me, quick! — it's important."

But the under-porter was one of those individuals who, by reason of constitutional peculiarities, absolutely refuse to be stirred or hurried. He was dusting a marble-topped table, and he deliberately finished his job before replying.

"All I know," he said at last, shaking out his duster with a flourish, "is that Number 55 and his lady come down at a quarter past eight or thereabouts and went off — in a taxicab — from that there door!"

"Do you know where they went?" demanded Credding. "Did you hear any address given when they got in?"

"I didn't go out with 'em," replied the man. "The night porter was on duty then — he saw them off."

"Well, where is the night porter?" asked Credding, with growing impatience. "Fetch him here — get him at once!"

The uniformed man, who was obviously the hall-porter, and who had stood by listening with y interest and sizing up Credding and his companion, stepped forward.

"The night porter's gone off duty, sir," he remarked. "He goes off at eight-thirty. Is it —" he paused, giving Credding a sagacious and knowing look — "police business, sir?"

"That's about it!" said Credding. "Look here, I must be on the track of those two! Where is that night porter to be found?"

"He lives in some dwellings close by," said the man. "I can send for him — he'll not be many minutes."

"Get him here as sharp as you can!" exclaimed Credding. "Every minute's of importance!" He turned and ran down the steps into the street, beckoning to Wendover and Orridge. "Too late!" he growled, as they hurried towards him. "Come!"

Orridge's keen face fell. His jaw, which was naturally long and pronounced, dropped, and his mouth opened.

"Can't have gone!" he exclaimed. "Weren't to be called till nine!"

"You'll learn something yet, young fellow!" retorted Credding. "That'll be — never to take your eyes off a hole when you've once seen a mouse go into it! To be called at nine! — all bluff, probably. You should never have left the hotel!"

"How the devil was I to communicate with anybody if I didn't?" demanded Orridge. "And I believe they did mean nine! — I should say something's happened that I don't know about. I know they went to their room as soon as they got in and didn't come out again — I saw a waiter take 'em some supper and drinks up there with my own eyes. And then I got a room myself, not so far off."

"Thinking they were caged till nine o'clock this morning!" said Credding satirically. "Well, my lad, it'll be a bit of news for you to hear that Colinrake was at High Barnet at or about half-past eleven last night —"

"That's all rot!" asserted Orridge hotly. "Colinrake was safe in this hotel at half-past eleven."

"Colinrake was ten miles away at half-past eleven, young fellow!" interrupted Credding. "That's where Colinrake was at that time, as I happen to know! And I wish to God I knew where he is now!"

He turned, motioning Wendover to follow him, back to the hall of the hotel and approached the man in uniform who by this time was deeply interested.

"Got him?" he asked.

"Be here in a minute, sir," replied the man. "Under porter's hurried for him. He'll come in by that other door — lives across that street."

Credding, followed by Wendover, walked across to the opposite entrance: the detective looked out, down the street indicated.

"This delay is the very devil!" he exclaimed, turning to Wendover. "Those two are off! — and Colinrake's so devilishly clever that if he once gets a fair start we'll have the utmost difficulty in coming up with him! And he was in time to get one or other of the Continental boat trains this morning."

"Better wire to the ports," advised Wendover. "Dover — Newhaven — Folkestone —"

"We'll see this night-porter first," said Credding. "We've time to get to Victoria and the other stations in readiness for those trains if we can only get an idea where these two went. You see —"

The night-porter, marshalled by the phlegmatic underling, came hurrying in at the door. Credding immediately drew him aside.

"Look here!" he said. "This is a police business — Scotland Yard; you understand? I want to know all about those two people who were in Number 55 last night — you saw them off this morning. What can you tell?"

The night-porter, a wideawake sort of fellow, nodded his comprehension of the situation.

"They came in here last night — it would be about ten," he answered. "No luggage — two fair-sized handbags. They got Number 55 and paid in advance for it — I showed them up. They ordered some supper up there and told me to call them at nine this morning — I marked the board for nine. But about half an hour after that, a wire arrived for Mr. Campbell — that was the name they'd booked — and I sent it up to 55. A few minutes later the gentleman came down in a hurry and asked where he could get a taxi. I told him — just outside. He hurried off and then turned back. 'I suppose you're on duty all night?' he said. 'Till eight-thirty in the morning, sir' says I. 'I may be back in a couple of hours,' he says. 'And I mayn't be back till three or four o'clock — I suppose I can get in any time?' 'Any time, sir,' I says."

"What time did he come back?" asked Credding.

"It would be about two o'clock," replied the night porter. "He came back in the same cab — I saw his driver through the glass doors there, and I can put you on to him — he's a man who's always on this stand."

"All right — in time," said Credding. "But Campbell — did he say or do anything when he got in?"

"He asked if I could get him a drink. I got him a whisky and soda. He seemed either tired or a bit excited — there was something — and when he'd drunk it he had another Then he told me that he wanted to alter his arrangements as he and his wife must leave at eight-fifteen prompt. I asked him about breakfast; he said no, they'd breakfast on the train —"

"Say what train — or line?" interrupted Credding.

"He didn't, sir! He went off then," continued the night porter. "Just before a quarter-past eight he and the young lady came down, carrying their handbags. I got them a taxi at this entrance — it was one that was passing. And off they went!"

"But where — what station — or what address?" demanded Credding. "That's what we want to know, badly!"

"Ah, but that's just what I can't tell you, sir!" answered the night porter. "For I don't know. He gave the address to the driver himself, and gave it in a low voice — I didn't catch it. And I don't know that driver — he's not a man who comes round here. But I can show you the other one I spoke of — if he's on the rank."

"Come on, then!" said Credding. "Try to find him!"

He hurried out into the street after the night porter, Wendover and the others following. The night porter went along the ranks of the taxicab drivers in the middle of the street, and suddenly catching sight of the man he wanted, beckoned to him.

"Here, Jim!" he said, as the man came up, "here's a gentleman wants to ask you some questions about that fare you had last night from our place — detective!" he added in a whisper, giving the man a warning wink. "After that man you drove!"

Credding caught the last words as he came up, and he went straight to business.

"Where did you drive that man last night?" he asked. "You picked him up outside the hotel about half-past ten and you brought him back to the hotel at two o'clock this morning. Where had you been with him in the meantime?"

The taxicab driver answered promptly.

"Drove him first to Shaftesbury Avenue — about half-way down," he answered. "He went into some flats. Waited for him — maybe five to ten minutes. Then to High Barnet. Pulled me up on the roadside there and told me to wait. He went a bit farther along and turned in at the gate of a house. After a bit he comes back again and stood by the side of the cab as if he was a-considering what to do next. A car comes along — from London way — a two-seater, and it passes my cab and turns in at that gate where he'd been. He told me to wait a bit longer and went back towards this here gate. He was away about ten minutes that time. Then he came back again and told me to go back to London, to Trafalgar Square. When we got close there he ordered me to pull up at the West Strand Post Office, and he went in there and was there some time — ten minutes, I should think. Then I drove him back here."

"That's all you can tell?" asked Credding.

"All I can tell you!" said the man. "Ain't no more to tell."

Credding drew Wendover aside.

"He's got the start of us, undoubtedly," he said. "And we shall do no good making any more inquiries here. I shall try that post office — and then we must get to the Yard and see what can be done. There's one thing we'll do now, and that's to send three other chaps to the stations from which the Continental boat-trains are starting within these next two hours — they can at any rate look out there. Tell your clerk to join in at it."

Dispatching one of the detectives to Charing Cross, another to London Bridge, and Orridge to Victoria, Credding chartered the cabman he had just talked to, and ushering Wendover into the cab, gave orders to be set down at the West Strand Post Office. Once on the way he took off his hat and wiped his forehead. "Phew!" he exclaimed. "Makes me warm, that, Mr. Wendover. Excitement! But, I fear it'll come to a sharp end. Colinrake's off — with that girl — and with whatever proceeds the two of 'em have got out of this. And the worst of it — for us — is this: Colinrake is evidently such an astute chap that he's probably made the most careful preparations for getting away. You know, it's all jolly well to talk about the way in which fellows like me spread a net round the escaping criminal and carefully draw him into it! That's all bosh! Such-like do get caught in the net now and then, but as often as not they slip clean away from it. When all's said and done, Mr. Wendover, a sharp man can get away from justice pretty easily if he plans it carefully — and gets a good start! That good start is the main point — and Colinrake's got one."

"There are the telegraph wires, you know," remarked Wendover quietly.

"Aye, I know, I know!" agreed Credding. "And uncommonly useful the telegraph — and the telephone — is, but you might wire a faithful description of a man to every railway station and every seaport in England, and then not get him. Look at this, now!" he went on, waving his hand at the streets through which they were passing, crowded with people hurrying to business. "Here's hundreds and thousands all around us, and they're only hundreds and thousands amongst millions — seven millions! — and we... want just one man! One man amongst millions of men!"

"Don't forget that the man's got a very striking young woman with him!" suggested Wendover.

"I don't forget! But even then it's a stiff job — unless they boldly present themselves, at once, at one of the stations we've sent to, or shall watch during the day, or at one of the ports we shall wire to. And I think Colinrake's too sharp for that!"

"What do you think he will do?" asked Wendover.

"I think he'll have done one of two things," said Credding. "He's either gone straight off — he'd be in time, I believe, to get an early train to Dover; I fancy there's one at nine o'clock that he'd certainly have time to catch — and I shall wire to Dover to see if he has — or he's made for the country, to some place where he can lie quiet for a bit and get away later. Still, there's another thing he may be doing."

"What's that?" asked Wendover.

"Hiding himself in the safest hiding-place in the world!" answered Credding with a knowing chuckle. "That's what!"

"And what is that?" inquired Wendover.

"This!" exclaimed Wendover, once more waving his hand at the crowded streets. "London, sir, London! God bless me! — I'd guarantee to hide myself in London any time in such a fashion that I'd defy all the men of my profession that ever walked into Scotland Yard or out of it to find me — I would so! That is, if I'd always plenty of ready money And Colinrake has!"

The cab pulled up at the Trafalgar Square end of the Strand, and Credding hurried into the post office with Wendover at his heels. And there came delay. Responsible officials had to be unearthed and interviewed and proffered reasons and explanations;

Credding's credentials to be examined and Scotland Yard telephoned to — nearly an hour had gone by before things materialised. The detective utilised that hour in wiring to Dover and Folkestone and Newhaven — as an afterthought he duplicated his message to Harwich, Liverpool and Southampton.

"That's making good use of our time, anyway," he remarked as he finished. "It may be of some use. When we know more..."

A clerk emerged from an inner door with a sheet of paper in his hand and approached Credding.

"This is a copy of the wire you wish to see," he said. "Dispatched from this office at one-thirty-five this morning."

He laid the paper down and the detective and Wendover bent over it. Credding slowly muttered the wording.

Goree Water Street Liverpool.

Please reserve for Mr. and Mrs. L. Campbell two first-class passages Liverpool to Buenos Ayres in Royal Mail Pacific s.s. Demerara sailing to-morrow.

Credding folded up the paper with something like an air of triumph, and with a word of thanks to the clerk, went back to the waiting cab and told the driver to go on to Scotland Yard.

"Got 'em!" he exclaimed as he settled back in his seat with a sigh of relief. "Got 'em as safe as safe can be! There's always a brick goes loose in the structures these chaps build! Now if Colinrake had never sent that wire, if he'd just —"

Wendover, staring out of the window as the cab turned into Whitehall, suddenly started and clutched the detective's arm.

"Credding!" he exclaimed. "There *is* Colinrake!"

Chapter XXVII
The Passport Office

Credding twisted sharply in his seat as the solicitor's hand gripped his arm.

"Where?" he exclaimed. "Where?"

"There!"— do you see? There! — passing in front of the Horse Guards! Look! — that's Colinrake, dead certain!"

Credding looked out of the right-hand window. It was a gloomy November morning and there was a considerable amount of yellow fog in the London streets; it lay along Whitehall and down Parliament Street in wisps. And out of one of these, on the opposite pavement, emerged the man that Credding wanted.

Colinrake was alone, and walking swiftly. Whatever he might have carried away with him from the hotel they had recently quitted, he was carrying nothing now but a carefully rolled umbrella. He was dressed in his usual careful fashion; there was nothing to distinguish him from the similarly attired, professional-looking men amongst whom he strode alone — he looked like many another well-groomed man going to his office. But as both men watching him well knew, Colinrake was not going to his office — he was going from it.

Credding looked; made sure; and quietly letting down the left-hand window, bade the driver pull up to the pavement. He motioned Wendover to follow him out.

"This fog's a godsend!" he said, when he had paid the driver and they moved down the street. "We'll be able to keep him in view easily from this side of the road. Now, Mr. Wendover, we'll separate! You go across — cautiously. Keep behind him — twenty yards or so — but keep your eye on him, and be careful about his slipping in anywhere. I'll stay this side — you can trust me to watch him from here. As long as he keeps on foot, we're safe of him: if he boards a bus or hails a cab or enters a station, we make for him at once. See!"

Wendover nodded and went slantingly across the road, keeping an eye on the hunted man. It seemed to him from Colinrake's jaunty and confident air that he had no idea whatever of being followed. He looked neither to right nor left and never round; wherever it was that he was going, he was making straight there. And down Whitehall he marched, and down Parliament Street, and then turned, and with Wendover in pursuit from one direction, and Credding from another, made his way to Queen Anne's Gate Buildings, and then walked direct, without a turn of the head, into the Passport Office.

Wendover stopped short in his pursuit when he saw that, and Credding, who had seen it too, came hurrying up to him.

"You saw where he went?" he exclaimed. "Might have guessed where he was bound, if I'd only thought! All right! — I've had business in that office before, and if I know anything he'll be safe enough for a bit! — they take their time there. Of course, he's gone to get the passports for himself and the girl! — probably applied for 'em some days ago. Now, Mr. Wendover, you keep a watch on that door while I run round to Scotland Yard and get help: I shan't be many minutes. If he comes out and makes off, summon that policeman over there and give him in charge! — tell the policeman we're coming. But I guess I shall be back before he's out — anyway, don't let him slip."

He hurried off, and Wendover, excited and anxious, remained near the door of the building into which Colinrake had gone. He looked speculatively at the policeman at whom Credding had pointed — certainly he was close at hand if wanted, and not very far away he saw another. And he saw still another in another direction, and there were men passing and re-passing — it would not be a difficult matter to detain Colinrake if he had to tackle him single-handed.

A few minutes went by; from Big Ben, high overhead in the dull sky, eleven o'clock struck. Nothing happened — except that a young man, in a fur-collared coat, with the collar turned up and his hat drawn down, and little more than an unusually pale face showing, came along, glanced at the door of the Passport Office, and checking his walk, began to loaf on the street a few yards away. He glanced furtively at Wendover, then at the door; it seemed to Wendover that he had a purpose in coming there....

Suddenly a closed travelling car, with a good deal of luggage showing, came round a corner, passed the loafer, passed Wendover, and drew up a few yards from the office door. Wendover had glanced sharply at it as it passed and had seen in it a woman, evidently warmly clad in furs, sitting back in a corner. He got a mere glimpse of her face and fancied he had seen it before. Then remembrance came sharply to him, and he knew that the woman was the girl he had seen in the witness-box at Brighton....

That instant Colinrake appeared at the door of the Passport Office, some papers in his hand. He glanced straight for the car, made for it had his hand on the door when Wendover started into activity and went quickly up to him.

"Mr. Colinrake," he began. "You cannot —"

Colinrake had the door open by that time, and one foot on the step. He turned on Wendover with a snarl as the solicitor beckoned to the policeman at the corner.

"Damn you!" he growled. "Take yourself off! What —"

The next words were drowned in a sharp, horrified scream from the woman inside the car, mingled with a frightened shout from the man near by.

"Look out! Look out! — he's shooting!"

Wendover never knew exactly what happened in that terrible half-minute. He heard a bang close by him, and heard Colinrake suddenly groan and saw him collapse where he stood, sliding from the door of the car to the pavement; he heard another and felt something strike himself smartly somewhere between his neck and shoulder; a third, and the girl's piercing screams suddenly cease — and then, all of a sudden, in a babel of voices and hurry of feet, everything grew dark before his eyes, and he felt himself dropping down, down...

And when next Wendover realised anything, he found himself in bed in the Westminster Hospital, with nurses in attendance, and, talking to a white-coated doctor in the background, Credding. He motioned to the nearest nurse.

"I remember now," he said faintly. "Ask the doctor to let me see Credding."

The nurse looked a gentle disapproval, but the doctor after coming across to the bedside, motioned the detective to follow him.

"You may talk to him for a minute or two," he said. "It'll set his mind at rest. But he mustn't talk."

Credding bent over the bed.

"Awfully grieved about this, Mr. Wendover!" he murmured. "Done nothing but blame myself ever since, though you're in no danger — all right again in a few days, they say. I never anticipated anything of the sort! It was that fellow the girl used to dance with — Sparre! Jealousy! He's done for 'em, Mr. Wendover! He killed Colinrake at that first shot; hit you in the shoulders in firing the second at the girl. But he shot her through the head at the third! Oh, yes, she's dead, poor thing! The fellow tried to shoot himself, too, but a couple of men who ran up got him in time. Half mad he is, I should say."

He paused for a moment, glancing at the doctor; then went on.

"They were off to Liverpool by road, those two," he continued. "We found no end of money, securities, and all that sort of thing on Colinrake or in his luggage, money and jewellery in the girl's belongings that must amount to thousands. So that's that! — and I think it clears Worthington — I think his account of everything was correct. There's no doubt Colinrake killed Severfield —"

The doctor tapped Credding's shoulder.

"That's enough!" he said.

Printed in Great Britain
by Amazon

58719678R00119